THE HAPPY FAMILY

THE HAPPY FAMILY

BERTHA MUZZY BOWER (B.M. SINCLAIR)

ISBN: 978-93-5344-232-3

First Published: -

LECTOR HOUSE

LECTOR HOUSE LLP
E-MAIL: lectorpublishing@gmail.com

"A MAN'S PLUMB CRAZY TO GO ROUND BLATTING ALL HE KNOWS"

THE HAPPY FAMILY

BY

B.M. BOWER (B.M. SINCLAIR)

AUTHOR OF
"Chip of the Flying U," "The Range Dwellers,"
"Her Prairie Knight," "The Lure of the Dim Trails,"
"The Lonesome Trail," "The Long Shadow," Etc.

THE HAPPY FAMILY.

TO B.W.V.

" ...met the Ananias of the cow camp. I have knocked about cow camps, mining camps, railroad and telegraph camps, and kicked up alkali dust for many a weary mile on the desert. Yet wherever I went I never failed to meet him. He is part and parcel of every outfit.... He is indispensable, irresistible, and incorrigible; and while in but few cases can he be held a thing of beauty, he is certainly a joy forever—at least to those who have known his type with some degree of understanding...."

From a letter.

CONTENTS

THE HAPPY FAMILY

ANANIAS GREEN

Pink, because he knew well the country and because Irish, who also knew it well, refused pointblank to go into it again even as a rep, rode alone except for his horses down into the range of the Rocking R. General roundup was about to start, down that way, and there was stock bought by the Flying U which ranged north of the Bear Paws.

It so happened that the owner of the Rocking R was entertaining a party of friends at the ranch; it also happened that the friends were quite new to the West and its ways, and they were intensely interested in all pertaining thereto. Pink gathered that much from the crew, besides observing much for himself. Hence what follows after.

Sherwood Branciforte was down in the blacksmith shop at the Rocking R, watching one Andy Green hammer a spur-shank straight. Andy was what he himself called a tamer of wild ones, and he was hard upon his riding gear. Sherwood had that morning watched with much admiration the bending of that same spur-shank, and his respect for Andy was beautiful to behold.

"Lord, but this is a big, wild country," he was saying enthusiastically, "and the people in it are big and—"

"Wild," supplied Andy. "Yes, you've just about got us sized up correct." He went on hammering, and humming under his breath, and thinking that, while admiration is all right in its time and place, it is sometimes a bit wearisome.

"Oh, but I didn't mean that," the young man protested. "What I meant was breezy and picturesque. Things can happen, out here. Life and men don't run in grooves."

"No, nor horses," assented Andy. "Leastways, not in oiled ones." He was remembering how that spur-shank had become bent.

"You did some magnificent riding, this morning. By Jove! I've never seen anything like it. Strange that one can come out here into a part of the country absolutely new and raw, and see things—"

"Oh, it ain't so raw as you might think," Andy defended jealously, "nor yet new."

"Of course it is new! A commonwealth in the making. You can't," he asserted triumphantly, "point to anything man-made that existed a hundred years ago; scarcely fifty, either. Your civilization is yet in the cradle—a lusty infant, and a—er—vociferous one, but still an infant in swaddling clothes." Sherwood Branciforte had given lectures before the Y.M.C.A. of his home town, and young ladies had spoken of him as "gifted," and he had come to hear of it, and to believe.

Andy Green squinted at the shank before he made reply. Andy, also, was "gifted," in his modest Western way.

"A country that can now and then show the papers for a civilization old as the Phenixes of Egypt," he said, in a drawling tone that was absolutely convincing, "ain't what I'd call raw." He decided that a little more hammering right next the rowel was necessary, and bent over the anvil solicitously. Even the self-complacency of Sherwood Branciforte could not fail to note his utter indifference to the presence and opinions of his companion. Branciforte was accustomed to disputation at times—even to enmity; but not to indifference. He blinked. "My dear fellow, do you realize what it is that statement might seem to imply?" he queried haughtily.

Andy, being a cowpuncher of the brand known as a "real," objected strongly both to the term and the tone. He stood up and stared down at the other disapprovingly. "I don't as a general thing find myself guilty of talking in my sleep," he retorted, "and I'm prepared to let anything I say stand till the next throw. We may be some vociferous, out here twixt the Mississippi and the Rockies, but we ain't no infant-in-the-cradle, Mister. We had civilization here when the Pilgrim Fathers' rock wasn't nothing but a pebble to let fly at the birds!"

"Indeed!" fleered Sherwood Branciforte, in a voice which gave much intangible insult to one's intelligence.

Andy clicked his teeth together, which was a symptom it were well for the other to recognize but did not. Then Andy smiled, which was another symptom. He fingered the spur absently, laid it down and reached, with the gesture that betrays the act as having become second nature, for his papers and tobacco sack.

"Uh course, you mean all right, and you ain't none to blame for what you don't know, but you're talking wild and scattering. When you stand up and tell me I can't point to nothing man-made that's fifty years old, or a hundred, you make me feel sorry for yuh. I can take you to something—or I've seen something—that's older than swearing; and I reckon that art goes back to when men wore their hair long and a sheep-pelt was called ample for dress occasions."

"Are you crazy, man?" Sherwood Branciforte exclaimed incredulously.

"Not what you can notice. You wait whilst I explain. Once last fall I was riding by my high lonesome away down next the river, when my horse went lame on me from slipping on a shale bank, and I was set afoot. Uh course, you being plumb ignorant of our picturesque life, you don't half know all that might signify to *imply*." This last in open imitation of Branciforte. "It implies that I was in one hell of a fix, to put it elegant. I was sixty miles from anywhere, and them sixty half the time standing on end and lapping over on themselves. That there is down where old mama Nature gave full swing to a morbid hankering after doing things un-conventional. Result is, that it's about as ungodly a mixture of nightmare scenery as this old world can show up; and I've ambled around considerable and am in a position to pass judgment.

"So there I was, and I wasn't in no mood to view the beauties uh nature to speak of; for instance, I didn't admire the clouds sailing around promiscous in the sky, nor anything like that. I was high and dry and the walking was about as poor as I ever seen; and my boots was high-heel and rubbed blisters before I'd covered a mile of that acrobatic territory. I wanted water, and I wanted it bad. Before I got it I wanted it a heap worse." He stopped, cupped his slim fingers around a match-blaze, and Branciforte sat closer. He did not know what was coming, but the manner of the indifferent narrator was compelling. He almost forgot the point at issue in the adventure.

"Along about dark, I camped for the night under a big, bare-faced cliff that was about as homelike and inviting as a charitable institution, and made a bluff at sleeping and cussed my bum luck in a way that wasn't any bluff. At sun-up I rose and mooched on." His cigarette needed another match and he searched his pockets for one.

"What about the—whatever it was you started to tell me?" urged Branciforte, grown impatient.

Andy looked him over calmly. "You've lived in ignorance for about thirty years or so—giving a rough guess at your age; I reckon you can stand another five minutes. As I was saying, I wandered around like a dogy when it's first turned loose on the range and is trying to find the old, familiar barn-yard and the skim-milk bucket. And like the dogy, I didn't run across anything that looked natural or inviting. All that day I perambulated over them hills, and I will say I wasn't enjoying the stroll none. You're right when you say things can happen, out here. There's some things it's just as well they don't happen too frequent, and getting lost and afoot in the Bad-lands is one.

"That afternoon I dragged myself up to the edge of a deep coulee and looked over to see if there was any way of getting down. There was a bright green streak down there that couldn't mean nothing but water, at that time of year; this was last fall. And over beyond, I could see the river that I'd went and lost. I looked and looked, but the walls looked straight as a Boston's man's pedigree. And then the sun come out from behind a cloud and lit up a spot that made me forget for a minute that I was thirsty as a dog and near starved besides.

"I was looking down on the ruins—and yet it was near perfect—of an old cas-tle. Every stone stood out that clear and distinct I could have counted 'em. There was a tower at one end, partly fell to pieces but yet enough left to easy tell what it was. I could see it had kinda loop-holes in it. There was an open place where I took it the main entrance had used to be; what I'd call the official entrance. But there was other entrances besides, and some of 'em was made by time and hard weather. There was what looked like a what-you-may-call-'em—a ditch thing, yuh mind, running around my side of it, and a bridge business. Uh course, it was all needing repairs bad, and part of it yuh needed to use your imagination on. I laid there for quite a spell looking it over and wondering how the dickens it come to be way down there. It didn't look to me like it ought to be there at all, but in a school geography or a history where the chapter is on historic and prehistoric hangouts uh the heathen."

"The deuce! A castle in the Bad-lands!" ejaculated Branciforte.

"That's what it was, all right. I found a trail it would make a mountain sheep seasick to follow, and I got down into the coulee. It was lonesome as sin, and spooky; but there was a spring close by, and a creek running from it; and what is a treat in that part uh the country, it was good drinking and didn't have neither alkali nor sulphur nor mineral in it. It was just straight water, and you can gamble I filled up on it a-plenty. Then I shot a rabbit or two that was hanging out around the ruins, and camped there till next day, when I found a pass out, and got my bearings by the river and come on into camp. So when you throw slurs on our plumb newness and shininess, I've got the cards to call yuh. That castle wasn't built last summer, Mister. And whoever did build it was some civilized. So there yuh are."

Andy took a last, lingering pull at the cigarette stub, flung it into the backened forge, and picked up the spur. He settled his hat on his head at its accustomed don't-give-a-darn tilt, and started for the door and the sunlight.

"Oh, but say! didn't you find out anything about it afterwards? There must have been something—"

"If it's relics uh the dim and musty past yuh mean, there was; relics to burn. I kicked up specimens of ancient dishes, and truck like that, while I was prowling around for fire-wood. And inside the castle, in what I reckon was used for the main hall, I run acrost a skeleton. That is, part of one. I don't believe it was all there, though."

"But, man alive, why haven't you made use of a discovery like that?" Branciforte followed him out, lighting his pipe with fingers that trembled. "Don't you realize what a thing like that means?"

Andy turned and smiled lazily down at him. "At the time I was there, I was all took up with the idea uh getting home. I couldn't eat skeletons, Mister, nor yet the remains uh prehistoric dishes. And I didn't run acrost no money, nor no plan marked up with crosses where you're supposed to do your excavating for treasure. It wasn't nothing, that I could see, for a man to starve to death while he examined it thorough. And so far as I know there ain't any record of it. I never heard no one mention building it, anyhow." He stooped and adjusted the spur to his heel to see if it were quite right, and went off to the stable humming under his breath.

Branciforte stood at the door of the blacksmith shop and gazed after him, puffing meditatively at his pipe. "Lord! the ignorance of these Western folk! To run upon a find like that, and to think it less important than getting home in time for supper. To let a discovery like that lie forgotten, a mere incident in a day's travel! That fellow thinks more, right now, about his horse going lame and himself raising blisters on his heels, than of—Jove, what ignorance! He—he couldn't *eat* the skeleton or the dishes! Jerusalem!" Branciforte knocked his pipe gently against the door-casing, put in into his coat pocket and hurried to the house to hunt up the others and tell them what he had heard.

That night the roundup pulled in to the home ranch.

The visitors, headed by their host, swooped down upon the roundup wagons just when the boys were gathered together for a cigarette or two apiece and a little talk before rolling in. There was no night-guarding to do, and trouble winged afar. Sherwood Branciforte hunted out Andy Green where he lay at ease with head and shoulders propped against a wheel of the bed-wagon and gossiped with Pink and a few others.

"Look here, Green," he said in a voice to arrest the attention of the whole camp, "I wish you'd tell the others that tale you told me this afternoon—about that ruined castle down in the hills. Mason, here, is a newspaper man; he scents a story for his paper. And the rest refuse to believe a word I say."

"I'd hate to have a rep like that, Mr. Branciforte," Andy said commiserating-ly, and turned his big, honest gray eyes to where stood the women—two breezy young persons with sleeves rolled to tanned elbows and cowboy hats of the mu-sical comedy brand. Also they had gay silk handkerchiefs knotted picturesque-ly around their throats. There was another, a giggly, gurgly lady with gray hair fluffed up into a pompadour. You know the sort. She was the kind who refuses to grow old, and so merely grows imbecile.

"Do tell us, Mr. Green," this young old lady urged, displaying much gold by her smile. "It sounds so romantic."

"It's funny you never mentioned it to any of us," put in the "old man" suspi-ciously.

Andy pulled himself up into a more decorous position, and turned his eyes towards his boss. "I never knew yuh took any interest in relic-hunting," he ex-plained mildly.

"Sherwood says you found a *skeleton!*" said the young old lady, shuddering pleasurably.

"Yes, I did find one—or part of one," Andy admitted reluctantly.

"What were the relics of pottery like?" demanded one of the cowboy-hatted girls, as if she meant to test him. "I do some collecting of that sort of thing."

Andy threw away his cigarette, and with it all compunction. "Well, I wasn't so much interested in the dishes as in getting something to eat," he apologized. "I saw several different kinds. One was a big, awkward looking thing and was pretty heavy, and had straight sides. Then I come across one or two more that was orna-mented some. One had what looked like a fish on it, and the other I couldn't make out very well. They didn't look to be worth much, none of 'em."

"Green," said his employer steadily, "*was* there such a place?"

Andy returned his look honestly. "There was, and there is yet, I guess," he asserted. "I'll tell you how you can find it and what it's like—if yuh doubt my words." He glanced around and found every man, including the cook, listening intently. He picked a blade of new grass and began splitting it into tiny threads. The host found boxes for the women to sit upon, and the men sat down upon the grass.

"Before I come here to work, I was riding for the Circle C. One day I was riding away down in the Bad-lands alone and my horse slipped in some shale rock and went lame; strained his shoulder so I couldn't ride him. That put me afoot, and climbing up and down them hills I lost my bearings and didn't know where I was at for a day or two. I wandered around aimless, and got into a strip uh country that was new to me and plumb lonesome and wild. "That second day is when I happened across this ruin. I was looking down into a deep, shut-in coulee, hunting water, when the sun come out and shone straight on to this place. It was right down under me; a stone ruin, with a tower on one end and kinda tumbled down so it wasn't so awful high—the tower wasn't. There was a—a—"

"Moat," Branciforte suggested.

"That's the word—a moat around it, and a bridge that was just about gone to pieces. It had loopholes, like the pictures of castles, and a—"

"Battlement?" ventured one of the musical-comedy cowgirls.

Andy had not meant to say battlement; of a truth, his conception of battlements was extremely hazy, but he caught up the word and warmed to the subject. "Battlement? well I should guess yes! There was about as elegant a battlement as I'd want to see anywhere. It was sure a peach. It was—" he hesitated for a fraction of a second. "It was high as the tower, and it had figures carved all over it; them kind that looks like kid-drawing in school, with bows and arrows stuck out in front of 'em, threatening."

"Not the old Greek!" exclaimed one of the girls in a little, breathless voice.

"I couldn't say as to that," Andy made guarded reply. "I never made no special study of them things. But they was sure old. And—"

"About how large was the castle?" put in the man who wrote things. "How many rooms, say?"

"I'd hate to give a guess at the size. I didn't step it off, and I'm a punk guesser. The rooms I didn't count. I only explored around in the main hall, like, a little. But it got dark early, down in there, and I didn't have no matches to waste. And next morning I started right out at sun-up to find the way home. No, I never counted the rooms, and if I had, the chances are I'd have likely counted the same one more'n once; to count them rooms would take an expert, which I ain't—not at counting. I don't reckon, though, that there was so awful many. Anyway, not more than fifteen or twenty. But as I say, I couldn't rightly make a guess, even; or I'd hate to. Ruins don't interest me much, though I was kinda surprised to run acrost that one, all right, and I'm willing to gamble there was warm and exciting times down there when the place was in running order. I'd kinda like to have been down there then. Last fall, though, there wasn't nothing to get excited over, except getting out uh there."

"A castle away out here! Just think, good people, what that means! Romance, adventure and scientific discoveries! We must go right down there and explore the place. Why can't we start at once—in the morning? This gentleman can guide us to the place, and—"

"It ain't easy going," Andy remarked, conscientiously. "It's pretty rough; some places, you'd have to walk and lead your horses."

They swept aside the discouragement.

"We'd need pick and shovels, and men to dig," cried one enthusiast. "Uncle Peter can lend us some of his men. There may be treasure to unearth. There may be *anything* that is wonderful and mysterious. Get busy, Uncle Peter, and get your outfit together; you've boasted that a roundup can beat the army in getting under way quickly, now let us have a practical demonstration. We want to start by six o'clock—all of us, with a cook and four or five men to do the excavating. Bring it to pass!" It was the voice of the girl whom her friends spoke of as "The life of the party;" the voice of the-girl-who-does-things.

"It's sixty-five miles from here, good and strong—and mostly up and down," put in Andy.

"'Quoth the raven,'" mocked the-girl-who-does-things. "We are prepared to face the ups-and-downs. Do we start at six, Uncle Peter?"

Uncle Peter glanced sideways at the roundup boss. To bring it to pass, he would be obliged to impress the roundup cook and part of the crew. It was breaking an unwritten law of the rangeland, and worse, it was doing something unbusiness-like and foolish. But not even the owner of the Rocking R may withstand the pleading of a pretty woman. Uncle Peter squirmed, but he promised:

"We start at six; earlier if you say so."

The roundup boss gave his employer a look of disgust and walked away; the crew took it that he went off to some secluded place to swear.

Thereafter there was much discussion of ways and means, and much enthusiasm among the visitors from the East—equalled by the depression of the crew, for cowboys do not, as a rule, take kindly to pick and shovel, and the excavators had not yet been chosen from among them. They were uneasy, and they stole frequent, betraying glances at one another. All of which amused Pink much. Pink would like to have gone along, and would certainly have offered his services, but for the fact that his work there was done and he would have to start back to the Flying U just as soon as one of his best saddle horses, which had stepped on a broken beer bottle and cut its foot, was able to travel. That would be in a few days, probably. So Pink sighed and watched the preparations enviously.

Since he was fairly committed into breaking all precedents, uncle Peter plunged recklessly. He ordered the mess-wagon to be restocked and prepared for the trip, and he took the bed-tent and half the crew. The foreman he wisely left behind with the remnant of his outfit. They were all to eat at the house while the mess-wagon was away, and they were to spread their soogans—which is to say beds—where they might, if the bunk-house proved too small or too hot.

The foreman, outraged beyond words, saddled at daybreak and rode to the nearest town, and the unchosen half turned out in a body to watch the departure of the explorers, which speaks eloquently of their interest; for cowboys off duty are prone to sleep long.

Andy, as guide, bolted ahead of the party that he might open the gate. Bolted is a good word, for his horse swerved and kept on running, swerved again, and came down in a heap. Andy did not get up, and the women screamed. Then Pink and some others hurried out and bore Andy, groaning, to the bunk-house.

The visitors from the East gathered, perturbed, around the door, sympathetic and dismayed. It looked very much as if their exploration must end where it began, and the-girl-who-does-things looked about to weep, until Andy, still groaning, sent Pink out to comfort them.

"He says you needn't give up the trip on his account," Pink announced musically from the doorway. "He's drawing a map and marking the coulee where the ruin is. He says most any of the boys that know the country at all can find the place for yuh. And he isn't hurt permanent; he strained his back so he can't ride, is all." Pink dimpled at the young old lady who was admiring him frankly, and withdrew.

Inside, Andy Green was making pencil marks and giving the chosen half explicit directions. At last he folded the paper and handed it to one called Sandy.

"That's the best I can do for yuh," he finished. "I don't see how yuh can miss it if yuh follow that map close. And if them gay females make any kick on the trail, you just remind 'em that I said all along it was rough going. So long, and good luck."

So with high-keyed, feminine laughter and much dust, passed the exploring party from the Rocking R.

"Say," Pink began two days later to Andy, who was sitting on the shady side of the bunk-house staring absently at the skyline, "There's a word uh praise I've been aiming to give yuh. I've seen riding, and I've done a trifle in that line myself, and learned some uh the tricks. But I want to say I never did see a man flop his horse any neater than you done that morning. I'll bet there ain't another man in the outfit got next your play. I couldn't uh done it better myself. Where did you learn that? Ever ride in Wyoming?"

Andy turned his eyes, but not his head—which was a way he had—and regarded Pink slantwise for at least ten seconds. "Yes, I've rode in Wyoming," he answered quietly. Then: "What's the chance for a job, up your way? Is the Flying U open for good men and true?"

"It won't cost yuh a cent to try," Pink told him. "How's your back? Think you'll be able to ride by the time Skeeker is able to travel?"

Andy, grinned. "Say," he confided suddenly, "if that hoss don't improve some speedy, I'll be riding on ahead. I reckon I'll be able to travel before them explorers get back, my friend."

"Why?" dimpled Pink boldly.

"Why? Well, the going is some rough, down that way. If they get them wagons half way to the coulee marked with a cross, they'll sure have to attach wings onto 'em. I've been some worried about that. I don't much believe uncle Peter is going to enjoy that trip—and he sure does get irritable by spells. I've got a notion to ride for some other outfit, this summer."

"Was that the reason you threw your horse down and got hurt, that morning?" questioned Pink, and Andy grinned again by way of reply.

"They'll be gone a week, best they can do," he estimated aloud. "We ought to be able to make our getaway by then, easy."

Pink assured him that a week would see them headed for the Flying U.

It was the evening of the sixth day, and the two were packed and ready to leave in the morning, when Andy broke off humming and gave a snort of dismay. "By gracious, there they come. My mother lives in Buffalo, Pink, in a little drab house with white trimmings. Write and tell her how her son— Oh, beloved! but they're hitting her up lively. If they made the whole trip in that there frame uh mind, they could uh gone clean to Miles City and back. How pretty the birds sing! Pink, you'll hear words, directly."

Directly Pink did.

"You're the biggest liar on earth," Sherwood Branciforte contributed to the recriminating wave that near engulfed Andy Green. "You sent us down there on a wild-goose chase, you brute. You—"

"I never sent nobody," Andy defended. "You was all crazy to go."

"And nothing but an old stone hut some trapper had built!" came an indignant, female tone. "There never was any castle, nor—"

"A man's home is his castle," argued Andy, standing unabashed before them. "Putting it that way, it was a castle, all right."

There was babel, out of which—

"And the skeleton! Oh, you—it was a dead *cow!*" This from the young old lady, who was looking very draggled and not at all young.

"I don't call to mind ever saying it was human," put in Andy, looking at her with surprised, gray eyes.

"And the battlements!" groaned the-girl-who-does-things.

"You wanted battlements," Andy flung mildly into the uproar. "I always aim to please." With that he edged away from them and made his escape to where the cook was profanely mixing biscuits for supper. All-day moves put an edge to his temper. The cook growled an epithet, and Andy passed on. Down near the stable he met one of the chosen half, and the fellow greeted him with a grin. Andy stopped abruptly.

"Say, they don't seem none too agreeable," he began tentatively, jerking his thumb toward the buzzing group. "How about it, Sandy? Was they that petulant all the way?"

Sandy, the map-bearer, chuckled. "It's lucky you got hurt at the last minute! And yet it was worth the trip. Uh course we got stalled with the wagons, the second day out, but them women was sure ambitious, and made us go on with a packadero layout. I will say that, going down, they stood the hardships remarkable. It was coming back that frazzled the party.

"And when we found the place—say, but it was lucky you wasn't along! They sure went hog-wild when they seen the ruins. The old party with the pompadoor displayed temper, and shed tears uh rage. When she looked into the cabin and seen the remains uh that cow-critter, there was language it wasn't polite to overhear. She said a lot uh things about you, Andy. One thing they couldn't seem to get over, and that was the smallness uh the blamed shack. Them fourteen or fifteen rooms laid heavy on their minds."

"I didn't say there was fourteen or fifteen rooms. I said I didn't count the rooms; I didn't either. I never heard of anybody counting one room. Did you, Pink?"

"No," Pink agreed, "I never did!"

Sandy became suddenly convulsed. "Oh, but the funniest thing was the ancient pottery," he gasped, the tears standing in his eyes. "That old Dutch oven was bad enough; but when one uh the girls—that one that collects old dishes—happened across an old mackerel can and picked it up and saw the fish on the label, she was the maddest female person I ever saw in my life, barring none. If you'd been in reach about that time, she'd just about clawed your eyes out, Andy Green. Oh me, oh my!" Sandy slapped his thigh and had another spasm.

Sounds indicated that the wave of recrimination was rolling nearer. Andy turned to find himself within arm's length of Uncle Pete.

"Maybe this is your idea of a practical joke, Green," he said to Andy. "But anyway, it will cost you your job. I ought to charge you up with the time my outfit has spent gallivanting around the country on the strength of your wild yarn. The quicker you hit the trail, the better it will suit me. By the way, what's your first name?" He asked, pulling out a check-book.

"Andy," answered the unrepentant one.

"Andy," Uncle Peter paused with a fountain pen between his fingers. He looked Andy up and down, and the frown left his face. He proceeded to write out the check, and when it was done he handed it over with a pleased smile.

"What did you do it for, Green?" he queried in a friendlier tone.

"Self-defence," Andy told him laconically, and turned away.

Half an hour later, Andy and Pink trailed out of the coulee that sheltered the Rocking R. When they were out and away from the fence, and Pink's horses, knowing instinctively that they were homeward bound, were jogging straight west without need of guidance, Andy felt in his pocket for cigarette material. His fingers came in contact with the check Uncle Peter had given him, and he drew it forth and looked it over again.

"Well, by gracious!" he said to himself. "Uncle Peter thinks we're even, I guess."

He handed the check to Pink and rolled his cigarette; and Pink, after one comprehending look at the slip of paper, doubled up over his saddle-horn and shouted with glee—for the check was written: "Pay to the order of Ananias Green."

"And I've got to sign myself a liar, or I don't collect no money," sighed Andy. "That's what I call tough luck, by gracious!"

BLINK

The range-land was at its unpicturesque worst. For two days the wind had raged and ranted over the hilltops, and whooped up the long coulees, so that tears stood in the eyes of the Happy Family when they faced it; impersonal tears blown into being by the very force of the wind. Also, when they faced it they rode with bodies aslant over their saddle-horns and hats pulled low over their streaming eyes, and with coats fastened jealously close. If there were buttons enough, well and good; if not, a strap cinched tightly about the middle was considered pretty lucky and not to be despised. Though it was early September, "sour-dough" coats were much in evidence, for the wind had a chill way of searching to the very marrow—and even a good, sheepskin-lined "sour-dough" was not always protection sufficient.

When the third day dawned bleakly, literally blown piecemeal from out darkness as bleak, the Happy Family rose shiveringly and with sombre disapproval of whatever met their blood-shot eyes; dressed hurriedly in the chill of flapping tent and went out to stagger drunkenly over to where Patsy, in the mess-tent, was trying vainly to keep the biscuits from becoming dust-sprinkled, and sundry pans and tins from taking jingling little excursions on their own account. Over the brow of the next ridge straggled the cavvy, tails and manes whipping in the gale, the nighthawk swearing so that his voice came booming down to camp. Truly, the day opened inauspiciously enough for almost any dire ending.

As further evidence, saddling horses for circle resolved itself, as Weary remarked at the top of his voice to Pink, at his elbow, into "a free-for-all broncho busting tournament." For horses have nerves, and nothing so rasps the nerves of man or beast as a wind that never stops blowing; which means swaying ropes and popping saddle leather, and coat-tails flapping like wet sheets on a clothes line. Horses do not like these things, and they are prone to eloquent manifestations of their disapproval.

Over by the bed-wagon, a man they called Blink, for want of a better name, was fighting his big sorrel silently, with that dogged determination which may easily grow malevolent. The sorrel was at best a high-tempered, nervous beast, and what with the wind and the flapping of everything in sight, and the pitching of half-a-dozen horses around him, he was nearly crazed with fear in the abstract.

Blink was trying to bridle him, and he was not saying a word—which, in the general uproar, was strange. But Blink seldom did say anything. He was one of the aliens who had drifted into the Flying U outfit that spring, looking for work. Chip had taken him on, and he had stayed. He could ride anything in his string, and he was always just where he was wanted. He never went to town when the others clattered off for a few hours' celebration more or less mild, he never took part in any of the camp fun, and he never offended any man. If any offended him they did not know it unless they were observant; if they were, they would see his pale lashes wink fast for a minute, and they might read aright the sign and refrain from further banter. So Blink, though he was counted a good man on roundup, was left pretty much alone when in camp.

Andy Green, well and none too favorably known down Rocking R way, and lately adopted into the Happy Family on the recommendation of Pink and his own pleasing personality, looped the latigo into the holder, gave his own dancing steed a slap of the don't-try-to-run-any-whizzers-on-me variety, and went over to help out Blink.

Blink eyed his approach with much the same expression with which he eyed the horse. "I never hollered for assistance," he remarked grudgingly when Andy was at his elbow. "When I can't handle any of the skates in my string, I'll quit riding and take to sheep-herding." Whereupon he turned his back as squarely as he might upon Andy and made another stealthy grab for the sorrel's ears. (There is such a thing in the range-land as jealousy among riders, and the fame of Andy Green had gone afar.)

"All right. Just as you say, and not as I care a darn," Andy retorted, and went back to where his own mount stood tail to the wind. He did not in the least mind the rebuff; he really felt all the indifference his manner portrayed—perhaps even more. He had offered help where help was needed, and that ended it for him. It never occurred to him that Blink might feel jealous over Andy's hard-earned reputation as a "tamer of wild ones," or mistake his good nature for patronage.

Five minutes later, when Chip looked around comprehensively at the lot of them in various degrees of readiness; saw that Blink was still fighting silently for mastery of the sorrel and told Andy to go over and help him get saddled, Andy said nothing of having had his services refused, but went. This time, Blink also said nothing, but accepted in ungracious surrender the assistance thus thrust upon him. For on the range-land, unless one is in a mind to roll his bed and ride away, one does not question when the leader commands. Andy's attitude was still that of indifference; he really thought very little about Blink or his opinions, and the rapid blinking of the pale lashes was quite lost upon him.

They rode, eighteen ill-natured, uncomfortable cowboys, tumultuously away from the camp, where canvas bulged and swayed, and loose corners cracked like pistol shots, over the hill where even the short, prairie grass crouched and flattened itself against the sod; where stray pebbles, loosened by the ungentle tread of pitching hoofs, skidded twice as far as in calm weather. The gray sky bent threateningly above them, wind-torn into flying scud but never showing a hint of blue. Later there might be rain, sleet, snow—or sunshine, as nature might whimsically direct; but for the present she seemed content with only the chill wind that blew the very heart out of a man.

Whenever Chip pulled up to turn off a couple of riders that they might search a bit of rough country, his voice was sharp with the general discomfort. When men rode away at his command, it was with brows drawn together and vengeful heels digging the short-ribs of horses in quite as unlovely a mood as themselves.

Out at the end of the "circle," Chip divided the remainder of his men into two groups for the homeward drive. One group he himself led. The other owned Weary as temporary commander and galloped off to the left, skirting close to the foothills of the Bear Paws. In that group rode Pink and Happy Jack, Slim, Andy Green and Blink the silent.

"I betche we get a blizzard out uh this," gloomed Happy Jack, pulling his coat collar up another fraction of an inch. "And the way Chip's headed us, we got to cross that big flat going back in the thick of it; chances is, we'll git lost."

No one made reply to this; it seemed scarcely worth while. Every man of them rode humped away from the wind, his head drawn down as close to his shoulders as might be. Conversation under those conditions was not likely to become brisk.

"A fellow that'll punch cows for a living," Happy Jack asserted venomously after a minute, "had ought to be shut up somewheres. He sure ain't responsible. I betche next summer don't see me at it."

"Aw, shut up. We know you're feeble-minded, without you blatting it by the hour," snapped Pink, showing never a dimple.

Happy Jack tugged again at his collar and made remarks, to which no one paid the slightest attention. They rode in amongst the hills and narrow ridges dividing "draws" as narrow, where range cattle would seek shelter from the cutting blast that raked the open. Then, just as they began to realize that the wind was not quite such a raging torment, came a new phase of nature's unpleasant humor.

It was not a blizzard that descended upon them, though when it came rolling down from the hilltops it much resembled one. The wind had changed and brought fog, cold, suffocating, impenetrable. Yet such was the mood of them that no one said anything about it. Weary had been about to turn off a couple of men, but did not. What was the use, since they could not see twenty yards?

For a time they rode aimlessly, Weary in the lead. Then, when it grew no better but worse, he pulled up, just where a high bank shut off the wind and a tangle of brush barred the way in front.

"We may as well camp right here till things loosen up a little," he said. "There's no use playing blind-man's-buff any longer. We'll have some fire, for a change. Mama! this is sure beautiful weather!"

At that, they brightened a bit and hurriedly dismounted and hunted dry wood. Since they were to have a fire, the general tendency was to have a big one; so that when they squatted before it and held out cold, ungloved fingers to the warmth, the flames were leaping high into the fog and crackling right cheerily. It needed only a few puffs at their cigarettes to chase the gloom from their faces and put them in the mood for talk. Only Blink sat apart and stared moodily into the fire, his hands clasped listlessly around his knees, and to him they gave no attention. He was an alien, and a taciturn one at that. The Happy Family were accustomed to living clannishly, even on roundup, and only when they tacitly adopted a man, as they had adopted Pink and Irish and, last but not least important, Andy Green, did they take note of that man's mood and demand reasons for any surliness.

"If Slim would perk up and go run down a grouse or two," Pink observed pointedly, "we'd be all right for the day. How about it, Slim?"

"Run 'em down yourself," Slim retorted. "By golly, I ain't no lop-ear bird dog."

"The law's out fer chickens," Happy Jack remarked dolefully.

"Go on, Happy, and get us a few. You've got your howitzer buckled on," fleered Andy Green. Andy it was whose fertile imagination had so christened Happy Jack's formidable weapon.

"Aw, gwan!" protested Happy Jack.

"Happy looks like he was out for a rep," bantered Pink. "He makes me think uh the Bad Man in a Western play. All he needs is his hat turned up in front and his sleeves rolled up to his elbow, like he was killing hogs. Happy would make a dandy-looking outlaw, with that gun and that face uh his."

"Say, by golly, I bet that's what he's figurin' on doing. He ain't going to punch cows no more—I bet he's thinking about turning out."

"Well, when I do, you'll be the first fellow I lay for," retorted Happy, with labored wit.

"You never'd get a rep shooting at a target the size uh Slim," dimpled Pink. "Is that toy cannon loaded, Happy?"

"I betche yuh dassen't walk off ten paces and let me show yuh," growled Happy.

Pink made as if to rise, then settled back with a sigh. "Ten paces is farther than you could drive me from this fire with a club," he said. "And you couldn't see me, in this fog."

"Say, it *is* pretty solid," said Weary, looking around him at the blank, gray wall. "A fellow could sit right here and be a lot ignorant of what's going on around him. A fellow could—"

"When I was riding down in the San Simon basin," spoke up Andy, rolling his second cigarette daintily between his finger-tips, "I had a kinda queer experience in a fog, once. It was thick as this one, and it rolled down just about as sudden and unexpected. That's a plenty wild patch uh country—or it was when I was there. I was riding for a Spanish gent that kept white men as a luxury and let the greasers do about all the rough work—such as killing off superfluous neighbors, and running brands artistic, and the like. Oh, he was a gay mark, all right.

"But about this other deal: I was out riding alone after a little bunch uh hosses, one day in the fall. I packed my gun and a pair uh field glasses, and every time I rode up onto a mesa I'd take a long look at all the lower country to save riding it. I guess I'd prognosticated around like that for two or three hours, when I come out on a little pinnacle that slopes down gradual toward a neighbor's home ranch—

only the ranch itself was quite a ride back up the basin.

"I got off my horse and set down on a rock to build me a smoke, and was gazing off over the country idle, when I seen a rider come up out of a little draw and gallop along quartering-like, to pass my pinnacle on the left. You know how a man out alone like that will watch anything, from a chicken hawk up in the air to a band uh sheep, without any interest in either one, but just to have your eyes on something that's alive and moves.

"So I watched him, idle, while I smoked. Pretty soon I seen another fellow ride out into sight where the first one had, and hit her up lively down the trail. I didn't do no wondering—I just sat and watched 'em both for want uh something better to do."

"Finding them strays wasn't important, I s'pose?" Happy Jack insinuated.

"It could wait, and did. So I kept an eye on these gazabos, and pretty soon I saw the hind fellow turn off the trail and go fogging along behind a little rise. He come into sight again, whipping down both sides like he was heading a wild four-year-old; and that was queer, because the only other live thing in sight was man number one, and I didn't see no reason why he should be hurting himself to get around to windward like that.

"Maybe it was five minutes I watched 'em: number one loping along like there wasn't nothing urgent and he was just merely going somewhere and taking his time for it, and number two quirting and spurring like seconds was diamonds."

"I wish they was that valuable to you," hinted Pink.

"They ain't, so take it easy. Well, pretty soon they got closer together, and then number two unhooked something on his saddle that caught the light. There's where I got my field glasses into play. I drew a bead with 'em, and seen right off it was a gun. And I hadn't no more than got my brain adjusted to grasp his idea, when he puts it back and takes down his rope. That there," Andy added naïvely, "promised more real interest; guns is commonplace.

"I took down the glasses long enough to size up the layout. Glasses, you know, are mighty deceiving when it comes to relative distances, and a hilltop a mile back looks, through the glass, like just stepping over a ditch. With the naked eye I could see that they were coming together pretty quick, and they done so.

"Number one looks back, but whether he seen number two I couldn't say; seemed to me like he just glanced back casual and in the wrong direction. Be that is it may, number two edged off a little and rode in behind a bunch uh mesquite— and then I seen that the trail took a turn, right there. So he pulled up and stood still till the other one had ambled past, and then he whirled out into the trail and swung his loop.

"When I'd got the glasses focused on 'em again, he had number one snared, all right, and had took his turns. The hoss he was riding—it was a buckskin—set back and yanked number one end over end out uh the saddle, and number one's hoss stampeded off through the brush. Number two dug in his spurs and went hell-bent off the trail and across country dragging the other fellow—and him bouncing over the rough spots something horrible.

"I don't know what got the matter uh me, then; I couldn't do anything but sit there on my rock and watch through the glasses. Anyway, while they looked close enough to hit with a rock, they was off a mile or more. So while I could see it all I couldn't do nothing to prevent. I couldn't even hear number one yell—supposing he done any hollering, which the chances is he did a plenty. It was for all the world like one uh these moving pictures.

"I thought it was going to be a case uh dragging to death, but it wasn't; it looked to me a heap worse. Number two dragged his man a ways—I reckon till he was plumb helpless—and then he pulled up and rode back to where he laid. The fellow tried to get up, and did get partly on his knees—and number one standing over him, watching.

"What passed I don't know, not having my hearing magnified like my sight was. I framed it up that number two was getting his past, present and future read out to him—what I'd call a free life reading. The rope was pinning his arms down to his sides, and number two was taking blamed good care there wasn't any slack, so fast as he tried to get up he was yanked back. From first to last he never had a ghost of a show.

"Then number two reaches back deliberate and draws his gun and commences shooting, and I commences hollering for him to quit it—and me a mile off and can't do nothing! I tell yuh right now, that was about the worst deal I ever went up against, to set there on that pinnacle and watch murder done in cold blood, and me plumb helpless.

"The first shot wasn't none fatal, as I could see plainer than was pleasant. Looked to me like he wanted to string out the agony. It was a clear case uh butchery from start to finish; the damnedest, lowest-down act a white man could be guilty of. He empties his six-gun—counting the smoke-puffs—and waits a minute, watching like a cat does a gopher. I was sweating cold, but I kept my eyes glued to them glasses like a man in a nightmare.

"When he makes sure the fellow's dead, he rides alongside and flips off the rope, with the buckskin snorting and edging off—at the blood-smell, I reckon. While he's coiling his rope, calm as if he'd just merely roped a yearling, the buckskin gets his head, plants it and turns on the fireworks.

"When that hoss starts in pitching, I come alive and drop the glasses into their case and make a jump for my own hoss. If the Lord lets me come up with that devil, I aim to deal out a case uh justice on my own hook; I was in a right proper humor for doing him like he done the other fellow, and not ask no questions. Looked to me like he had it coming, all right.

"I'd just stuck my toe in the stirrup, when down comes the fog like a wet blanket on everything. I couldn't see twenty feet—" Andy stopped and reached for a burning twig to relight his cigarette. The Happy Family was breathing hard with the spell of the story.

"Did yuh git him?" Happy Jack asked hoarsely. Andy took a long puff at his cigarette. "Well, I— Holy smoke! what's the matter with *you*, Blink?" For Blink was leaning forward, half crouched, like a cat about to pounce, and was glaring fixedly at Andy with lips drawn back in a snarl. The Happy Family looked, then stared.

Blink relaxed, shrugged his shoulders and grinned unmirthfully. He got up, pulled up his chaps with the peculiar, hitching gesture which comes with long practice and grows to be second nature, and stared back defiantly at the wondering faces lighted by the dancing flames. He turned his back coolly upon them and walked away to where his horse stood, took up the reins and stuck his toe in the stirrup, went up and landed in the saddle ready for anything. Then he wheeled the big sorrel so that he faced those at the camp-fire.

"A man's a damned fool, Andy Green, to see more than is meant for him to see. He's plumb crazy to go round blatting all he knows. You won't tell that tale again, *mi amigo!*"

There was the pop of a pistol, a puff of blue against the gray, and then the fog reached out and gathered Blink and the sorrel to itself. Only the clatter of galloping hoofs came to them from behind the damp curtain. Andy Green was lying on his back in the grass, his cigarette smoking dully in his fingers, a fast widening red streak trailing down from his temple.

The Happy Family rose like a covey of frightened chickens before the echoes were done playing with the gun-bark. On the heels of Blink's shot came the crack of Happy Jack's "howitzer" as he fired blindly toward the hoof-beats. There was more shooting while they scurried to where their horses, snorting excitement, danced uneasily at the edge of the bushes. Only one man spoke, and that was Pink, who stopped just as he was about to swing into the saddle.

"Damme for leaving my gun in camp! I'll stay with Andy. Go on—and if yuh don't get him, I'll—" he turned back, cursing hysterically, and knelt beside the long figure in the grass. There was a tumult of sound as the three raced off in pursuit, so close that the flight of the fugitive was still distinct in the fog.

While they raced they cursed the fog that shielded from their vengeance their quarry, and made such riding as theirs a blind gamble with the chances all in favor of broken bones; their only comfort the knowledge that Blink could see no better than could they. They did not talk, just at first. They did not even wonder if Andy was dead. Every nerve, every muscle and every thought was concentrated upon the pursuit of Blink. It was the instant rising to meet an occasion undreamed of in advance, to do the only thing possible without loss of a second in parley. Truly, it were ill for Blink to fall into the hands of those three in that mood.

They rode with quirt and spur, guided only by the muffled *pluckety-pluck, pluckety-pluck* of Blink's horse fleeing always just before. Whenever the hoof-beats seemed a bit closer, Happy Jack would lift his long-barreled .45 and send a shot at random toward the sound. Or Weary or Slim would take a chance with their shorter guns. But never once did they pull rein for steep or gulley, and never once did the hoof-beats fail to come back to them from out the fog.

The chase had led afar and the pace was telling on their mounts, which breathed asthmatically. Slim, best he could do, was falling behind. Weary's horse stumbled and went to his knees, so that Happy Jack forged ahead just when the wind, puffing up from the open, blew aside the gray fog-wall. It was not a minute, nor half that; but it was long enough for Happy Jack to see, clear and close, Blink pausing irresolutely upon the edge of a deep, brush-filled gulley. Happy Jack gave a hoarse croak of triumph and fired, just as the fog-curtain swayed back maddeningly. Happy Jack nearly wept with pure rage. Weary and Slim came up, and together they galloped to the place, riding by instinct of direction, for there was no longer any sound to guide.

Ten minutes they spent searching the gulley's edge. Then they saw dimly, twenty feet below, a huddled object half-hidden in the brush. They climbed down none too warily, though they knew well what might be lying, venomous as a coiled rattler, in wait for them below. Slipping and sliding in the fog-dampened grass, they reached the spot, to find the big sorrel crumpled there, dead. They searched anxiously and futilely for more, but Blink was not there, nor was there anything to show that he had ever been there. Then not fear, perhaps, but caution, came to Happy Jack.

"Aw, say! he's got away on us—the skunk! He's down there in the brush, somewheres, waiting for somebody to go in and drag him out by the ear. I betche he's laying low, right now, waiting for a chance to pot-shot us. We better git back out uh this." He edged away, his eyes on the thicket just below. To ride in there was impossible, even to the Happy Family in whole or in part. To go in afoot was not at all to the liking of Happy Jack.

Slim gave a comprehensive, round-eyed stare at the unpromising surroundings, and followed Happy Jack. "By golly, that's right. Yuh don't git me into no hole like that," he assented.

Weary, foolhardy to the last, stayed longest; but even Weary could not but admit that the case was hopeless. The brush was thick and filled the gully, probably from end to end. Riding through it was impossible, and hunting it through on foot would be nothing but suicide, with a man like Blink hidden away in its depths. They climbed back to the rim, remounted and rode, as straight as might be, for the camp-fire and what lay beside, with Pink on guard.

It was near noon when, through the lightening fog, they reached the place and discovered that Andy, though unconscious, was not dead. They found, upon examination of his hurt, that the bullet had ploughed along the side of his head above his ear; but just how serious it might be they did not know. Pink, having a fresh horse and aching for action, mounted and rode in much haste to camp, that the bed-wagon might be brought out to take Andy in to the ranch and the ministrations of the Little Doctor. Also, he must notify the crew and get them out searching for Blink.

All that night and the next day the cowboys rode, and the next. They raked the foothills, gulley by gulley, their purpose grim. It would probably be a case of shoot-on-sight with them, and nothing saved Blink save the all-important fact that never once did any man of the Flying U gain sight of him. He had vanished completely after that fleeting glimpse Happy Jack had gained, and in the end the Flying U was compelled to own defeat.

Upon one point they congratulated themselves: Andy, bandaged as he was, had escaped with a furrow ploughed through the scalp, though it was not the fault of Blink that he was alive and able to discuss the affair with the others—more exactly, to answer the questions they fired at him.

"Didn't you recognize him as being the murderer?" Weary asked him curiously.

Andy moved uneasily on his bed. "No, I didn't. By gracious, you must think I'm a plumb fool!"

"Well, yuh sure hit the mark, whether yuh meant to or not," Pink asserted. "He was the jasper, all right. Look how he was glaring at yuh while you were telling about it. *He* knew he was the party, and having a guilty conscience, he naturally supposed yuh recognized him from the start."

"Well, I didn't," snapped Andy ungraciously, and they put it down to the peevishness of invalidism and overlooked the tone.

"Chip has given his description in to the sheriff," soothed Weary, "and if he gets off he's sure a good one. And I heard that the sheriff wired down to the San Simon country and told 'em their man was up here. Mama! What bad breaks a man will make when he's on the dodge! If Blink had kept his face closed and acted normal, nobody would have got next. Andy didn't know he was the fellow that done it. But it sure was queer, the way the play come up. Wasn't it, Andy?"

Andy merely grunted. He did not like to dwell upon the subject, and he showed it plainly.

"By golly! he must sure have had it in for that fellow," mused Slim ponderously, "to kill him the way Andy says he did. By golly, yuh can't wonder his eyes stuck out when he heard Andy telling us all about it!"

"I betche he lays for Andy yet, and gits him," predicted Happy Jack felicitously. "He won't rest whilst an eye-witness is running around loose. I betche he's cached in the hills right now, watching his chance."

"Oh, go to hell, the whole lot of yuh!" flared Andy, rising to an elbow. "What the dickens are yuh roosting around here for? Why don't yuh go on out to camp where yuh belong? You're a nice bunch to set around comforting the sick! *Vamos*, darn yuh!"

Whereupon they took the hint and departed, assuring Andy, by way of farewell, that he was an unappreciative cuss and didn't deserve any sympathy or sick-calls. They also condoled openly with Pink because he had been detailed as nurse, and advised him to sit right down on Andy if he got too sassy and haughty over being shot up by a real outlaw. They said that any fool could build himself a bunch of trouble with a homicidal lunatic like Blink, and it wasn't anything to get vain over.

Pink slammed the door upon their jibes and offered Andy a cigarette he had just rolled; not that Andy was too sick to roll his own, but because Pink was notably soft-hearted toward a sick man and was prone to indulge himself in trifling attentions.

"Yuh don't want to mind that bunch," he placated. "They mean all right, but they just can't help joshing a man to death."

Andy accepted also a light for the cigarette, and smoked moodily. "It ain't their joshing," he explained after a minute "It's puzzling over what I can't understand that gets on my nerves. I can't see through the thing, Pink, no way I look at it."

"Looks plain enough to me," Pink answered. "Uh course, it's funny Blink should be the man, and be setting there listening—"

"Yes, but darn it all, Pink, there's a funnier side to it than that, and it's near driving me crazy trying to figure it out. Yuh needn't tell anybody, Pink, but it's like this: I was just merely and simply romancing when I told that there blood-curdling tale! I never was south uh the Wyoming line except when I was riding in a circus and toured through, and that's the truth. I never was down in the San Simon basin. I never set on no pinnacle with no field glasses—" Andy stopped short his labored confession to gaze, with deep disgust, upon Pink's convulsed figure. "Well," he snapped, settling back on the pillow, "*laugh*, darn yuh! and show your ignorance! By gracious, I wish *I* could see the joke!" He reached up gingerly and readjusted the bandage on his head, eyed Pink sourly a moment, and with a grunt eloquent of the mood he was in turned his face to the wall.

MISS MARTIN'S MISSION

When Andy Green, fresh-combed and shining with soap and towel polish, walked into the dining-room of the Dry Lake Hotel, he felt not the slightest premonition of what was about to befall. His chief sensation was the hunger which comes of early rising and of many hours spent in the open, and beyond that he was hoping that the Chinaman cook had made some meat-pie, like he had the week before. His eyes, searching unobtrusively the long table bearing the unmistakable signs of many other hungry men gone before—for Andy was late—failed to warn him. He pulled out his chair and sat down, still looking for meat-pie.

"Good after*noon!*" cried an eager, feminine voice just across the table.

Andy started guiltily. He had been dimly aware that some one was sitting there, but, being occupied with other things, had not given a thought to the sitter, or a glance. Now he did both while he said good afternoon with perfunctory politeness.

"Such a *beauti*ful day, isn't it? *so* invigorating, like rare, old wine!"

Andy assented somewhat dubiously; it had never just struck him that way; he thought fleetingly that perhaps it was because he had never come across any rare, old wine. He ventured another glance. She was not young, and she wore glasses, behind which twinkled very bright eyes of a shade of brown. She had unpleasantly regular hair waves on her temples, and underneath the waves showed streaks of gray. Also, she wore a black silk waist, and somebody's picture made into a brooch at her throat. Further, Andy dared not observe. It was enough for one glance. He looked again for the much-desired meat-pie.

The strange lady ingratiatingly passed him the bread. "You're a cowboy, aren't you?" was the disconcerting question that accompanied the bread.

"Well, I—er—I punch cows," he admitted guardedly, his gaze elsewhere than on her face.

"I *knew* you were a cowboy, the moment you entered the door! I could tell by the tan and the straight, elastic walk, and the silk handkerchief knotted around your throat in that picturesque fashion. (Oh, I'm older than you, and dare speak as I think!) I've read a great deal about cowboys, and I do admire you all as a type of free, great-hearted, noble manhood!"

Andy looked exactly as if someone had caught him at something exceedingly foolish. He tried to sugar his coffee calmly, and so sent it sloshing all over the saucer.

"Do you live near here?" she asked next, beaming upon him in the orthodox, motherly fashion.

"Yes, ma'am, not very near," he was betrayed into saying—and she might make what she could of it. He had not said "ma'am" before since he had gone to school.

"Oh, I've heard how you Western folks measure distances," she teased. "About how many miles?"

"About twenty."

"I suppose that is not far, to you knights of the plains. At home it would be called a *dreadfully* long journey. Why, I have known numbers of old men and women who have never been so far from their own doors in their lives! What would you think, I wonder, of their little forty acre farms?"

Andy had been brought to his sixteenth tumultuous birthday on a half-acre in the edge of a good-sized town, but he did not say so. He shook his head vaguely and said he didn't know. Andy Green, however, was not famous for clinging ever to the truth.

"You out here in this great, wide, free land, with the free winds ever blowing and the clouds—"

"Will you pass the butter, please?" Andy hated to interrupt, but he was hungry.

The strange lady passed the butter and sent with it a smile. "I have read and heard so much about this wild, free life, and my heart has gone out to the noble fellows living their lonely life with their cattle and their faithful dogs, lying beside their camp-fires at night while the stars stood guard—"

Andy forgot his personal embarrassment and began to perk up his ears. This was growing interesting.

"—And I have felt how lonely they must be, with their rude fare and few pleasures, and what a field there must be among them for a great and noble work; to uplift them and bring into their lonely lives a broader, deeper meaning; to help them to help themselves to be better, nobler men and women—"

"We don't have any lady cowpunchers out here," interposed Andy mildly.

The strange lady had merely gone astray a bit, being accustomed to addressing Mothers' Meetings and the like. She recovered herself easily. "Nobler men, the bulwarks of our nation." She stopped and eyed Andy archly. Andy, having observed that her neck was scrawny, with certain cords down the sides that moved unpleasantly when she talked, tried not to look.

"I wonder if you can guess what brings me out here, away from home and friends! Can you guess?"

Andy thought of several things, but he could not feel that it would be polite to mention them. Agent for complexion stuff, for instance, and next to that, wanting a husband. He shook his head again and looked at his potato.

"You *can't guess*?" The tone was the one commonly employed for the encouragement, and consequent demoralization of, a primary class. Andy realized that he was being talked down to, and his combativeness awoke. "Well, away back in my home town, a woman's club has been thinking of all you lonely fellows, and have felt their hearts swell with a desire to help you—so far from home and mother's influence, with only the coarse pleasures of the West, and amid all the temptations that lie in wait—" She caught herself back from speech-making—"and they have sent *me*—away out here—to be your *friend*; to help you to help yourselves become better, truer men and—" She did not say women, though, poor soul, she came near it. "So, I am going to be your friend. I want to get in touch with you all, first; to win your confidence and teach you to look upon me in the light of a mother. Then, when I have won your confidence, I want to organize a Cowboys' Mutual Improvement and Social Society, to help you in the way of self-improvement and to resist the snares laid for homeless boys like you. Don't you think I'm very— *brave*?" She was smiling at him again, leaning back in her chair and regarding him playfully over her glasses.

"You sure are," Andy assented, deliberately refraining from saying "yes, ma'am," as had been his impulse.

"To come away out here—*all alone*—among all you wild cowboys with your guns buckled on and your wicked little mustangs—Are you sure you won't shoot me?"

Andy eyed her pityingly. If she meant it, he thought, she certainly was wabbly in her mind. If she thought that was the only kind of talk he could savvy, then she was a blamed idiot; either way, he felt antagonistic. "The law shall be respected in your case," he told her, very gravely.

She smiled almost as if she could see the joke; after which she became twitteringly, eagerly in earnest. "Since you live near here, you must know the Whitmores. Miss Whitmore came out here, two or three years ago, and married her brother's coachman, I believe—though I've heard conflicting stories about it; some have said he was an artist, and others that he was a jockey, or horse-trainer. I heard too that he was a cowboy; but Miss Whitmore certainly wrote about this young man driving her brother's carriage. However, she is married and I have a letter of introduction to her. The president of our club used to be a schoolmate of her mother. I shall stop with them—I have heard so much about the Western hospitality—and shall get into touch with my cowboys from the vantage point of proximity. Did you say you know them?"

"I work for them," Andy told her truthfully in his deep amazement, and immediately repented and wished that he had not been so virtuous. With Andy, to wish was to do—given the opportunity.

"Then I can go with you out to their farm—ranchero! How nice! And on the way you can tell me all about yourself and your life and hopes—because I do want to get in touch with you all, you know—and I'll tell you all my plans for you; I have some *beau*tiful plans! And we'll be very good friends by the time we reach our destination, I'm sure. I want you to feel from the start that I am a true friend, and that

I have your welfare very much at heart. Without the confidence of my cowboys, I can do nothing. Are there any more at home like you?"

Andy looked at her suspiciously, but it was so evident she never meant to quote comic opera, that he merely wondered anew. He struggled feebly against temptation, and fell from grace quite willingly. It isn't polite to "throw a load" at a lady, but then Andy felt that neither was it polite for a lady to come out with the avowed intention of improving him and his fellows; it looked to him like butting in where she was not wanted, or needed.

"Yes, ma'am, there's quite a bunch, and they're pretty bad. I don't believe you can do much for 'em." He spoke regretfully.

"Do they—*drink*?" she asked, leaning forward and speaking in the hushed voice with which some women approach a tabooed subject.

"Yes ma'am, they do. They're hard drinkers. And they"—he eyed her speculatively, trying to guess the worst sins in her category—"they play cards—gamble—and swear, and smoke cigarettes and—"

"All the more need of someone to help them overcome," she decided solemnly. "What you need is a coffee-house and reading room here, so that the young men will have some place to go other than the saloons. I shall see to that right away. And with the Mutual Improvement and Social Society organized and working smoothly, and a library of standard works for recreation, together with earnest personal efforts to promote temperance and clean-living, I feel that a *wonderful* work can be done. I saw you drive into town, so I know you can take me out with you; I hope you are going to start soon. I feel very impatient to reach the field and put my sickle to the harvest."

Andy mentally threw up his hands before this unshakable person. He had meant to tell her that he had come on horseback, but she had forestalled him. He had meant to discourage her—head her off, he called it to himself. But there seemed no way of doing it. He pushed back his chair and rose, though he had not tasted his pie, and it was lemon pie at that. He had some faint notion of hurrying out of town and home before she could have time to get ready; but she followed him to the door and chirped over his shoulder that it wouldn't take her two minutes to put on her wraps. Andy groaned.

He tried—or started to try—holding out at Rusty Brown's till she gave up in despair; but it occurred to him that Chip had asked him to hurry back. Andy groaned again, and got the team.

She did not wait for him to drive around to the hotel for her; possibly she suspected his intentions. At any rate, she came nipping down the street toward the stable just as he was hooking the last trace, and she was all ready and had a load of bags and bundles.

"I'm not going to begin by making trouble for you," she twittered. "I thought I could just as well come down here to the wagon as have you drive back to the hotel. And my trunk did not come on the train with me, so I'm all ready."

Andy, having nothing in mind that he dared say to a lady, helped her into the wagon.

At sundown or thereabouts—for the days were short and he had a load of various things besides care—Andy let himself wearily into the bunk-house where was assembled the Happy Family. He merely grunted when they spoke to him, and threw himself heavily down upon his bunk.

"For Heaven's sake, somebody roll me a cigarette! I'm too wore out to do a thing, and I haven't had a smoke since dinner," he groaned, after a minute.

"Sick?" asked Pink solicitously.

"Sick as a dog! water, water!" moaned Andy. All at once he rolled over upon his face and shook with laughter more than a little hysterical, and to the questioning of the Happy Family gave no answer but howls. The Happy Family began to look at one another uneasily.

"Aw, let up!" Happy Jack bellowed. "You give a man the creeps just to listen at yuh."

"I'm going to empty the water-bucket over yuh in a minute," Pink threatened, "Go get it, Cal; it's half full."

Andy knew well the metal of which the Happy Family was made, and the night was cool for a ducking. He rolled back so that they could see his face, and struggled for calm. In a minute he sat up and merely gurgled.

"Well, say, I had to do something or die," he explained, gasping. "I've gone through a heap, the last few hours, and I was right where I couldn't do a thing. By gracious, I struck the ranch about as near bug-house as a man can get and recover. Where's a cigarette?"

"What you've gone through—and I don't give a cuss what it is—ain't a marker for what's going to happen if yuh don't loosen up on the history," said Jack Bates firmly.

Andy smoked hungrily while he surveyed the lot. "How calm and innocent yuh all look," he observed musingly, "with your hats on and saying words that's rude, and smoking the vile weed regardless, never dreaming what's going to drop, pretty soon quick. Yuh make me think of a hymn-song my step-mother used to sing a lot, about 'They dreamed not of danger, those sinners of old, whom—'"

"Hand me the water bucket," directed Pink musically.

"Oh, well—take it from the shoulder, then; I was only trying to lead up to it gradual, but yuh *will* have it raw. You poor, dear cowboys, that live your lonely lives watching over your cattle with your *faithful dogs* and the stars for company, you're going to be *improved*. (You'll sure stand a lot of it, too!) A woman's relief club back East has felt the burden of your no-accountness and general orneriness, and has sent one of its leading members out here to reform yuh. You're going to be hazed into a Cowboys' Mutual Improvement and Social Society, and quit smoking cigarettes and cussing your hosses and laying over Rusty's bar when yuh ride into town; and for pleasure and recreation you're going to read Tennyson's poems, and when yuh get caught out in a blizzard yuh'll be heeled with Whittier's *Snowbound*, pocket edition. Emerson and Browning and Shakespeare and Gatty" (Andy misquoted; he meant Goethe) "and all them stiffs is going to be set before yuh regular and in your mind constant, purging it of unclean thoughts, and grammar is going to be learnt yuh as a side-line. Yuh—"

"Mama mine," broke in Weary. "I have thought sometimes, when Andy broke loose with that imagination uh his, that he'd gone the limit; but next time he always raises the limit out uh sight. He's like the Good Book says: he's prone to lie as the sparks fly-upward."

Andy gazed belligerently at the skeptical group. "I brought her out from town," he said doggedly, "and whilst I own up to having an imagination, she's stranger than fiction. She'd make the fellow that wrote "She" lay down with a headache. She's come out here to help us cowboys live nobler, better lives. She's going to learn yuh Browning, darn yuh! and Emerson and Gatty. She said so. She's going to fill your hearts with love for dumb creatures, so when yuh get set afoot out on the range, or anything like that, yuh won't put in your time cussing the miles between you and camp; you'll have a pocket edition of 'Much Ado About Nothing' to read, or the speech Mark Anthony made when he was running for office. Or supposing yuh left 'em all in camp, yuh'll study nature.

There's sermons in stones, she says. She's going to send for a pocket library that can easy be took on roundup—"

"Say, I guess that's about enough," interrupted Pink restlessly. "We all admit you're the biggest liar that ever come West of the Mississippi, without you laying it on any deeper."

Whereupon Andy rose in wrath and made a suggestive movement with his fist. "If I was romancing," he declared indignantly, "I'd do a smoother job; when I do lie, I notice yuh all believe it—till yuh find out different. And by gracious yuh might do as much when I'm telling the truth! Go up to the White House and see, darn yuh! If yuh don't find Miss Verbena Martin up there telling the Little Doctor how her heart goes out to her dear cowboys and how she's going to get in touch with 'em and help 'em lead nobler, better lives, you can kick me all round the yard. And I hope, by gracious, she *does* improve yuh! Yuh sure do need it a lot."

The Happy Family discussed the tale freely and without regard for the feelings of Andy; they even became heated and impolite, and they made threats. They said that a liar like him ought to be lynched or gagged, and that he was a disgrace to the outfit. In the end, however, they decided to go and see, just to prove to Andy that they knew he lied. And though it was settled that Weary and Pink should be the investigating committee, by the time they were halfway to the White House they had the whole Happy Family trailing at their heels. A light snow had begun to fall since dark, and they hunched their shoulders against it as they went. Grouped uncomfortably just outside the circle of light cast through the unshaded window, they gazed silently in upon Chip and the Little Doctor and J.G. Whitmore, and upon one other; a strange lady in a black silk shirtwaist and a gold watch suspended from her neck by a chaste, black silken cord; a strange lady with symmetrical waves in her hair and gray on her temples, and with glasses and an eager way of speaking.

She was talking very rapidly and animatedly, and the others were listening and stealing glances now and then at one another. Once, while they watched, the Little Doctor looked at Chip and then turned her face toward the window. She was biting her lips in the way the Happy Family had learned to recognize as a great desire to laugh. It all looked suspicious and corroborative of Andy's story, and the Happy Family shifted their feet uneasily in the loose snow.

They watched, and saw the strange lady clasp her hands together and lean forward, and where her voice had before come to them with no words which they could catch distinctly, they heard her say something quite clearly in her enthusiasm: "Eight real cowboys *here*, almost within reach! I must see them before I sleep! I must get in touch with them at once, and show them that I am a true friend. Come, Mrs. Bennett! Won't you take me where they are and let me meet my boys? for they *are* mine in spirit; my heart goes out to them—"

The Happy Family waited to hear no more, but went straightway back whence they had come, and their going savored of flight.

"Mama mine! she's coming down to the bunkhouse!" said Weary under his breath, and glanced back over his shoulder at the White House bulking large in the night. "Let's go on down to the stable and roost in the hay a while."

"She'll out-wind us, and be right there waiting when we come back," objected Andy, with the wisdom gained from his brief acquaintance with the lady. "If she's made up her mind to call on us, there's no way under Heaven to head her off."

They halted by the bunk-house door, undecided whether to go in or to stay out in the open.

"By golly, she don't improve *me*!" Slim asserted pettishly. "I hate books like strychnine, and, by golly, she can't make me read 'em, neither."

"If there's anything I do despise it's po'try," groaned Cal Emmett.

"Emerson and Browning and Shakespeare and *Gatty*," named Andy gloomily.

Whereat Pink suddenly pushed open the door and went in as goes one who knows exactly what he is about to do. They followed him distressfully and silently. Pink went immediately to his bunk and began pulling off his boots.

"I'm going to bed," he told them. "You fellows can stay up and entertain her if yuh want to—*I* won't!"

They caught the idea and disrobed hastily, though the evening was young. Irish blew out the lamp and dove under the blankets just as voices came faintly from up the hill, so that when Chip rapped a warning with his knuckles on the door, there was no sound within save an artificial snore from the corner where lay Pink. Chip was not in the habit of knocking before he entered, but he repeated the summons with emphasis.

"Who's there-e?" drawled sleepily a voice—the voice of Weary.

"Oh, I do believe they've retired!" came, in a perturbed feminine tone, to the listening ears of the Happy Family.

"Gone to bed?" cried Chip gravely.

"Hours ago," lied Andy fluently. "We're plumb wore out. What's happened?"

"Oh, don't disturb the poor fellows! They're tired and need their rest," came the perturbed tone again. After that the voices and the footsteps went up the hill again, and the Happy Family breathed freer. Incidentally, Pink stopped snoring and made a cigarette.

Going to bed at seven-thirty or thereabouts was not the custom of the Happy Family, but they stayed under the covers and smoked and discussed the situation. They dared not have a light, and the night was longer than they had ever known a night to be, for it was late before they slept. It was well that Miss Verbena Martin could not overhear their talk, which was unchivalrous and unfriendly in the extreme. The general opinion seemed to be that old maid improvers would better stay at home where they might possibly be welcome, and that when the Happy Family wanted improving they would let her know. Cal Emmett said that he wouldn't mind, if they had only sent a young, pretty one. Happy Jack prophesied plenty of trouble, and boasted that she couldn't haul *him* into no s'ciety. Slim declared again that by golly, she wouldn't do no improving on *him*, and the others— Weary and Irish and Pink and Jack Bates and Andy—discussed ways and means and failed always to agree. When each one hoots derision at all plans but his own, it is easy guessing what will be the result. In this particular instance the result was voices raised in argument—voices that reached Chip, grinning and listening on the porch of the White House—and tardy slumber overtaking a disgruntled Happy Family on the brink of violence.

It was not a particularly happy Family that woke to memory and a snowy Sunday; woke late, because of the disturbing evening. When they spoke to one another their voices were but growls, and when they trailed through the snow to their breakfast they went in moody silence.

They had just brightened a bit before Patsy's Sunday breakfast, which included hot-cakes and maple syrup, when the door was pushed quietly open and the Little Doctor came in, followed closely by Miss Martin; an apologetic Little Doctor, who seemed, by her very manner of entering, to implore them not to blame *her* for the intrusion. Miss Martin was not apologetic. She was disconcertingly eager and glad to meet them, and pathetically anxious to win their favor.

Miss Martin talked, and the Happy Family ate hurriedly and with lowered eyelids. Miss Martin asked questions, and the Happy Family kicked one another's shins under the table by way of urging someone to reply; for this reason there was a quite perceptible pause between question and answer, and the answer was invariably "the soul of wit"—according to that famous recipe. Miss Martin told them naively all about her hopes and her plans and herself, and about the distant woman's club that took so great an interest in their welfare, and the Happy Family listened dejectedly and tried to be polite. Also, they did not relish the hot-cakes as usual, and Patsy had half the batter left when the meal was over, instead of being obliged to mix more, as was usually the case.

When they had eaten, the Happy Family filed out decorously and went hastily down to the stables. They did not say much, but they did glance over their shoulders uneasily once or twice.

"The old girl is sure hot on our trail," Pink remarked when they were safely through the big gate. "She must uh got us mixed up with some Wild West show, in her mind. Josephine!"

"Well, by golly, she don't improve *me*," Slim repeated for about the tenth time.

The horses were all fed and everything tidy for the day, and several saddles were being hauled down significantly from their pegs, when Irish delivered himself of a speech, short but to the point. Irish had been very quiet and had taken no part in the discussion that had waxed hot all that morning.

"Now, see here," he said in his decided way. "Maybe it didn't strike you as anything but funny—which it sure is. But yuh want to remember that the old girl has come a dickens of a long ways to do us some good. She's been laying awake nights thinking about how we'll get to calling her something nice: Angel of the Roundup, maybe—you can't tell, she's that romantic. And right here is where I'm going to give the old girl the worth of her money. It won't hurt *us*, letting her talk wild and foolish at us once a week, maybe; and the poor old thing'll just be tickled to death thinking what a lot uh good she's doing. She won't stay long, and—well, I go in. If she'll feel better and more good to the world improving me, she's got my permission. I guess I can stand it a while."

The Happy Family looked at him queerly, for if there was a black sheep in the flock, Irish was certainly the man; and to have Irish take the stand he did was, to say the least, unexpected.

Cal Emmett blurted the real cause of their astonishment. "You'll have to sign the pledge, first pass," he said. "That's going to be the ante in *her* game. How—"

"Well, I don't play nobody's hand, or stake anybody's chips, but my own," Irish retorted, the blood showing under the tan on his cheeks.

"And we won't das't roll a cigarette, even, by golly!" reminded Slim. For Miss Martin, whether intentionally or not, had made plain to them the platform of the new society.

Irish got some deep creases between his eyebrows, and put back his saddle. "You can do as yuh like," he said, coldly. "I'm going to stay and go to meeting this afternoon, according to her invite. If it's going to make that poor old freak feel any better thinking she's a real missionary—" He turned and walked out of the stable without finishing the sentence, and the Happy Family stood quite still and watched him go.

Pink it was who first spoke. "I ain't the boy to let any long-legged son-of-a-gun like Irish hit a gait I can't follow," he dimpled, and took the saddle reluctantly off Toots. "If he can stand it, I guess I can."

Weary loosened his latigo. "If Cadwolloper is going to learn poetry, I will, too," he grinned. "Mama! it'll be good as a three-ringed circus! I never thought uh that, before. I couldn't miss it."

"Oh, well, if you fellows take a hand, I'll sure have to be there to see," Andy decided. "Two o'clock, did she say?"

"I hate to be called a quitter," Pink remarked dispiritedly to the Happy Family in general; a harassed looking Happy Family, which sat around and said little, and watched the clock. In an hour they would be due to attend the second meeting of the M.I.S.S.—and one would think, from the look of them, that they were about to be hanged. "I hate to be called a quitter, but right here's where I lay 'em down. The rest of yuh can go on being improved, if yuh want to—darned if I will, though. I'm all in."

"I don't recollect hearing anybody say we wanted to," growled Jack Bates. "Irish, maybe, is still burning with a desire to be nice and chivalrous; but you can count me out. One dose is about all I can stand."

"By golly, I wouldn't go and feel that foolish again, not if yuh paid me for it," Slim declared.

Irish grinned and reached for his hat. "I done my damnettest," he said cheerfully. "I made the old girl happy once; now, one Irish Mallory is due to have a little joy coming his way. I'm going to town."

> "'Break, break, break, on thy cold, gray crags, oh sea,
> And I would that my tongue could utter the thoughts that come
> over me.'

"You will observe, gentlemen, the beautiful sentiment, the euphonious rhythm, the noble—" Weary went down, still declaiming mincingly, beneath four irate bodies that hurled themselves toward him and upon him.

"We'll break, break, break every bone in your body if you don't shut up. You will observe the beautiful sentiment of *that* a while," cried Pink viciously. "I've had the euphonious rhythm of my sleep broke up ever since I set there and listened at her for two hours. Josephine!"

Irish stopped with his hand on the door knob. "I was the jay that started it," he admitted contritely. "But, honest, I never had a hunch she was plumb locoed; I thought she was just simply foolish. Come on to town, boys!"

Such is the power of suggestion that in fifteen minutes the Happy Family had passed out of sight over the top of the grade; all save Andy Green, who told them he would be along after a while, and that they need not wait. He looked at the clock, smoked a meditative cigarette and went up to the White House, to attend the second meeting of the Mutual Improvement and Social Society.

When he faced alone Miss Verbena Martin, and explained that the other members were unavoidably absent because they had a grudge against a man in Dry Lake and had gone in to lynch him and burn the town, Miss Martin was shocked into postponing the meeting. Andy said he was glad, because he wanted to go in and see the fight; undoubtedly, he assured her, there would be a fight, and probably a few of them would get killed off. He reminded her that he had told her right in the start that they were a bad lot, and that she would have hard work reforming them; and finally, he made her promise that she would not mention to anyone what he had told her, because it wouldn't be safe for him, or for her, if they ever got to hear of it. After that Andy also took the trail to town, and he went at a gallop and smiled as he rode.

Miss Martin reflected shudderingly upon the awful details of the crime, as hinted at by Andy, and packed her trunk. It might be brave and noble to stay and work among all those savages, but she doubted much whether it were after all her duty. She thought of many ways in which she could do more real good nearer home. She had felt all along that these cowboys were an untrustworthy lot; she had noticed them glancing at one another in a secret and treacherous manner, all through the last meeting, and she was positive they had not given her that full confidence without which no good can be accomplished. That fellow they called Happy looked capable of almost any crime; she had never felt quite safe in his presence.

Miss Martin pictured them howling and dancing around the burning dwellings of their enemies, shooting every one they could see; Miss Martin had imagination, of a sort. But while she pictured the horrors of an Indian massacre she continued to pack her suit-case and to consult often her watch. When she could do no more it occurred to her that she would better see if someone could take her to the station. Fortunately for all concerned, somebody could. One might go further and say that somebody was quite willing to strain a point, even, in order to get her there in time for the next train.

The Happy Family was gathered in Rusty Brown's place, watching Irish do things to a sheep-man from Lonesome Prairie, in a game of pool. They were just giving vent to a prolonged whoop of derision at the sheep-man's play, when a rig flashed by the window. Weary stopped with his mouth wide open and stared; leaned to the window and craned to see more clearly.

"Mama mine!" he ejaculated incredulously. "I could swear I saw Miss Verbena in that rig, with her trunk, and headed towards the depot. Feel my pulse, Cadwolloper, and see if I'm normal."

But Pink was on his way to the back door, and from there climbed like a cat to the roof of the coal-house, where, as he knew from experience, one could see the trail to the depot, and the depot itself.

"It's sure her," he announced. "Chip's driving like hell, and the smoke uh the train's just coming around the bend from the big field. Wonder what struck her so sudden?" He turned and looked down into the grinning face of Andy Green.

"She was real insulted because you fellows played hookey," Andy explained. "I tried to explain, but it didn't help none. I don't believe her heart went out to us like she claimed, anyhow."

HAPPY JACK, WILD MAN.

Happy Jack, over on the Shonkin range, saw how far it was to the river and mopped the heat-crimsoned face of him with a handkerchief not quite as clean as it might have been. He hoped that the Flying U wagons would be where he had estimated that they would be; for he was aweary of riding with a strange outfit, where his little personal peculiarities failed to meet with that large tolerance accorded by the Happy Family. He didn't think much of the Shonkin crew; grangers and pilgrims, he called them disgustedly in his mind. He hoped the Old Man would not send him on that long trip with them south of the Highwoods—which is what he was on his way to find out about. What Happy Jack was hoping for, was to have the Old Man—as represented by Chip—send one of the boys back with him to bring over what Flying U cattle had been gathered, together with Happy's bed and string of horses. Then he would ride with the Happy Family on the familiar range that was better, in his eyes, than any other range that ever lay outdoors—and the Shonkin outfit could go to granny. (Happy did not, however, say "granny").

He turned down the head of a coulee which promised to lead him, by the most direct route—if any route in the Badlands can be called direct—to the river, across which, and a few miles up on Suction Creek, he confidently expected to find the Flying U wagons. The coulee wound aimlessly, with precipitous sides that he could not climb, even by leading his horse. Happy Jack, under the sweltering heat of mid-June sunlight, once more mopped his face, now more crimson than ever, and relapsed into his habitual gloom. Just when he was telling himself pessimistically that the chances were he would run slap out on a cut bank where he couldn't get down to the river at all, the coulee turned again and showed the gray-blue water slithering coolly past, with the far bank green and sloping invitingly.

The horse hurried forward at a shuffling trot and thrust his hot muzzle into the delicious coolness. Happy Jack slipped off and, lying flat on his stomach, upstream from the horse, drank deep and long, then stood up, wiped his face and considered the necessity of crossing. Just at this point the river was not so wide as in others, and for that reason the current flowed swiftly past. Not too swiftly, however, if one took certain precautions. Happy Jack measured mentally the strength of the current and the proper amount of caution which it would be expedient to use, and began his preparations; for the sun was sliding down hill toward the western skyline, and he wished very much to reach the wagons in time for supper, if he could.

Standing in the shade of the coulee wall, he undressed deliberately, folding each garment methodically as he took it off. When the pile was complete to socks and boots, he rolled it into a compact bundle and tied it firmly upon his saddle. Stranger, his horse, was a good swimmer, and always swam high out of water. He hoped the things would not get very wet; still, the current was strong, and his characteristic pessimism suggested that they would be soaked to the last thread. So, naked as our first ancestor, he urged his horse into the stream, and when it was too deep for kicking—Stranger was ever uncertain and not to be trusted too far— he caught him firmly by the tail and felt the current grip them both. The feel of the water was glorious after so long a ride in the hot sun, and Happy Jack reveled in the cool swash of it up his shoulders to the back of his neck, as Stranger swam out and across to the sloping, green bank on the home side. When his feet struck bottom, Happy Jack should have waded also—but the water was so deliciously cool, slapping high up on his shoulders like that; he still floated luxuriously, towed by Stranger—until Stranger, his footing secure, glanced back at Happy sliding behind like a big, red fish, snorted and plunged up and on to dry land.

Happy Jack struck his feet down to bottom, stumbled and let go his hold of the tail, and Stranger, feeling the weight loosen suddenly, gave another plunge and went careering up the bank, snorting back at Happy Jack. Happy swore, waded out and made threats, but Stranger, seeing himself pursued by a strange figure whose only resemblance to his master lay in voice and profanity, fled in terror before him.

Happy Jack, crippling painfully on the stones, fled fruitlessly after, still shouting threats. Then, as Stranger, galloping wildly, disappeared over a ridge, he stood and stared stupidly at the place where the horse had last been seen. For the moment his mind refused to grasp all the horror of his position; he stepped gingerly over the hot sand and rocks, sought the shelter of a bit of overhanging bank, and sat dazedly down upon a rock too warm for comfort. He shifted uneasily to the sand beside, found that still hotter, and returned to the rock.

He needed to think; to grasp this disaster that had come so suddenly upon him. He looked moodily across to the southern bank, his chin sunken between moist palms, the while the water dried upon his person. To be set afoot, down here in the Badlands, away from the habitations of men and fifteen miles from the probable location of the Flying U camp, was not nice. To be set afoot *naked*—it was horrible, and unbelievable. He thought of tramping, barefooted and bare-legged, through fifteen miles of sage-covered Badlands to camp, with the sun beating down on his unprotected back, and groaned in anticipation. Not even his pessimism had ever pictured a thing so terrible.

He gazed at the gray-blue river which had caused this trouble that he must face, and forgetting the luxury of its coolness, cursed it venomously. Little waves washed up on the pebbly bank, and glinted in the sun while they whispered mocking things to him. Happy Jack gave over swearing at the river, and turned his wrath upon Stranger—Stranger, hurtling along somewhere through the breaks, with all Happy's clothes tied firmly to the saddle. Happy Jack sighed lugubriously when he remembered how firmly. A fleeting hope that, if he followed the trail of Stranger, he might glean a garment or two that had slipped loose, died almost before it lived. Happy Jack knew too well the kind of knots he always tied. His favorite boast that nothing ever worked loose on his saddle, came back now to mock him with its absolute truth.

The sun, dropping a bit lower, robbed him inch by inch of the shade to which he clung foolishly. He hunched himself into as small a space as his big frame would permit, and hung his hat upon his knees where they stuck out into the sunlight. It was very hot, and his position was cramped, but he would not go yet; he was still thinking—and the brain of Happy Jack worked ever slowly. In such an unheard-of predicament he felt dimly that he had need of much thought.

When not even his hat could shield him from the sun glare, he got up and went nipping awkwardly over the hot beach. He was going into the next river-bottom—wherever that was—on the chance of finding a cow-camp, or some cabin where he could, by some means, clothe himself. He did not like the idea of facing the Happy Family in his present condition; he knew the Happy Family. Perhaps he might find someone living down here next the river. He hoped so—for Happy Jack, when things were so bad they could not well be worse, was forced to give over the prediction of further evil, and pursue blindly the faintest whisper of hope. He got up on the bank, where the grass was kinder to his unaccustomed feet than were the hot stones below, and hurried away with his back to the sun, that scorched him cruelly.

In the next bottom—and he was long getting to it—the sage brush grew dishearteningly thick. Happy began to be afraid of snakes. He went slowly, stepping painfully where the ground seemed smoothest; he never could walk fifteen miles in his bare feet, he owned dismally to himself. His only hope lay in getting clothes.

Halfway down the bottom, he joyfully came upon a camp, but it had long been deserted; from the low, tumble-down corrals, and the unmistakable atmosphere of the place, Happy Jack knew it for a sheep camp. But nothing save the musty odor and the bare cabin walls seemed to have been left behind. He searched gloomily, thankful for the brief shade the cabin offered. Then, tossed up on the rafters and forgotten, he discovered a couple of dried sheep pelts, untanned and stiff, almost, as shingles. Still, they were better than nothing, and he grinned in sickly fashion at the find.

Realizing, in much pain, that some protection for his feet was an absolute necessity, he tore a pelt in two for sandals. Much search resulted in the discovery of a bit of rotted rope, which he unraveled and thereby bound a piece of sheepskin upon each bruised foot. They were not pretty, but they answered the purpose. The other pelt he disposed of easily by tying the two front legs together around his neck and letting the pelt hang down his back as far as it would reach. There being nothing more that he could do in the way of self-adornment, Happy Jack went out again into the hot afternoon. At his best, Happy Jack could never truthfully be called handsome; just now, clothed inadequately in gray Stetson hat and two meager sheepskins, he looked scarce human.

Cheered a bit, he set out sturdily over the hills toward the mouth of Suction Creek. The Happy Family would make all kinds of fools of themselves, he supposed, if he showed up like this; but he might not be obliged to appear before them in his present state of undress; he might strike some other camp, first. Happy Jack was still forced to be hopeful. He quite counted on striking another camp before reaching the wagons of the Flying U.

The sun slid farther and farther toward the western rim of tumbled ridges as Happy Jack, in his strange raiment, plodded laboriously to the north. The mantle he was forced to shift constantly into a new position as the sun's rays burned deep a new place, or the stiff hide galled his blistered shoulders. The sandals did better, except that the rotten strands of rope were continually wearing through on the bottom, so that he must stop and tie fresh knots, or replace the bit from the scant surplus which he had prudently brought along.

Till sundown he climbed toilfully up the steep hills and then scrambled as toilfully into the coulees, taking the straightest course he knew for the mouth of Suction Creek; that, as a last resort, while he watched keenly for the white flake against green which would tell of a tent pitched there in the wilderness. He was hungry—when he forgot other discomforts long enough to think of it. Worst, perhaps, was the way in which the gaunt sage brush scratched his unclothed legs when he was compelled to cross a patch on some coulee bottom. Happy Jack swore a great deal, in those long, heat-laden hours, and never did he so completely belie the name men had in sarcasm given him.

Just when he was given over to the most gloomy forebodings, a white square stood out for a moment sharply against a background of pines, far below him in a coulee where the sun was peering fleetingly before it dove out of sight over a hill. Happy Jack—of a truth, the most unhappy Jack one could find, though he searched far and long—stood still and eyed the white patch critically. There was only the one; but another might be hidden in the trees. Still, there was no herd grazing anywhere in the coulee, and no jingle of cavvy bells came to his ears, though he listened long. He was sure that it was not the camp of the Flying U, where he would be ministered unto faithfully, to be sure, yet where the ministrations would be mingled with much wit-sharpened raillery harder even to bear than was his present condition of sun-blisters and scratches. He thanked the Lord in sincere if unorthodox terms, and went down the hill in long, ungraceful strides.

It was far down that hill, and it was farther across the coulee. Each step grew more wearisome to Happy Jack, unaccustomed as he was to using his own feet as a mode of travel. But away in the edge of the pine grove were food and raiment, and a shelter from the night that was creeping down on him with the hurried stealth of a mountain lion after its quarry. He shifted the sheepskin mantle for the thousandth time; this time he untied it from his galled shoulders and festooned it modestly if unbecomingly about his middle.

Feeling sure of the unfailing hospitality of the rangeland, be the tent-dweller whom he might, Happy Jack walked boldly through the soft, spring twilight that lasts long in Montana, and up to the very door of the tent. A figure—a female figure—slender and topped by thin face and eyes sheltered behind glasses, rose up, gazed upon him in horror, shrieked till one could hear her a mile, and fell backward into the tent. Another female figure appeared, looked, and shrieked also—and even louder than did the first. Happy Jack, with a squawk of dismay, turned and flew incontinently afar into the dusk. A man's voice he heard, shouting inquiry; another, shouting what, from a distance, sounded like threats. Happy Jack did not wait to make sure; he ran blindly, until he brought up in a patch of prickly-pear, at which he yelled, forgetting for the instant that he was pursued. Somehow he floundered out and away from the torture of the stinging spines, and took to the hills. A moon, big as the mouth of a barrel, climbed over a ridge and betrayed him to the men searching below, and they shouted and fired a gun. Happy Jack did not believe they could shoot very straight, but he was in no mood to take chances; he sought refuge among a jumble of great, gray bowlders; sat himself down in the shadow and caressed gingerly the places where the prickly-pear had punctured his skin, and gave himself riotously over to blasphemy.

The men below were prowling half-heartedly, it seemed to him—as if they were afraid of running upon him too suddenly. It came to him that they were afraid of him—and he grinned feebly at the joke. He had not before stopped to consider his appearance, being concerned with more important matters. Now, however, as he pulled the scant covering of the pelt over his shoulders to keep off the chill of the night, he could not wonder that the woman at the tent had fainted. Happy Jack suspected shrewdly that he could, in that rig, startle almost any one.

He watched the coulee wistfully. They were making fires, down there below him; great, revealing bonfires at intervals that would make it impossible to pass their line unseen. He could not doubt that some one was *cached* in the shadows with a gun. There were more than two men; Happy Jack thought that there must be at least four or five. He would have liked to go down, just out of gun range, and shout explanations and a request for some clothes—only for the women. Happy was always ill at ease in the presence of strange women, and he felt, just now, quite unequal to the ordeal of facing those two. He sat huddled in the shadow of a rock and wished profanely that women would stay at home and not go camping out in the Badlands, where their presence was distinctly inappropriate and undesirable. If the men down there were alone, he felt sure that he could make them understand. Seeing they were not alone, however, he stayed where he was and watched the fires, while his teeth chattered with cold and his stomach ached with the hunger he could not appease.

Till daylight he sat there unhappily and watched the unwinking challenge of the flames below, and miserably wished himself elsewhere; even the jibes of the Happy Family would be endurable, so long as he had the comfort afforded by the Flying U camp. But that was miles away. And when daylight brought warmth and returning courage, he went so far as to wish the Flying U camp farther away than it probably was. He wanted to get somewhere, and ask help from strangers rather than those he knew best.

With that idea fixed in his mind, he got stiffly to his bruised feet, readjusted the sheepskin and began wearily to climb higher. When the sun tinged all the hilltops golden yellow, he turned and shook his fist impotently at the camp far beneath him. Then he went on doggedly.

Standing at last on a high peak, he looked away toward the sunrise and made out a white speck on a grassy side-hill; beside it, a gray square moved slowly over the green. Sheep, and a sheep camp—and Happy Jack, hater of sheep though he was, hailed the sight as a bit of rare good luck. His spirits rose immediately, and he started straight for the place.

Down in the next coulee—there were always coulees to cross, no matter in what direction one would travel—he came near running plump into three riders, who were Irish Mallory, and Weary, and Pink. They were riding down from the direction of the camp where were the women, and they caught sight of him immediately and gave chase. Happy Jack had no mind to be rounded up by that trio; he dodged into the bushes, and though they dug long, unmerciful scratches in his person, clung to the shelter they gave and made off at top speed. He could hear the others shouting at one another as they galloped here and there trying to locate him, and he skulked where the bushes were deepest, like a criminal in fear of lynching.

Luck, for once, was with him, and he got out into another brush-fringed coulee without being seen, and felt himself, for the present, safe from that portion of the Happy Family. Thereafter he avoided religiously the higher ridges, and kept the direction more by instinct than by actual knowledge. The sun grew hot again and he hurried on, shifting the sheepskin as the need impressed.

When at last he sighted again the sheep, they were very close. Happy Jack grew cautious; he crept down upon the unsuspecting herder as stealthily as an animal hunting its breakfast. Herders sometimes carry guns—and the experience of last night burned hot in his memory.

Slipping warily from rock to rock, he was within a dozen feet, when a dog barked and betrayed his presence. The herder did not have a gun. He gave a yell of pure terror and started for camp after his weapon. Happy Jack, yelling also, with long leaps followed after. Twice the herder looked over his shoulder at the weird figure in gray hat and flapping sheepskin, and immediately after each glance his pace increased perceptibly. Still Happy Jack, desperate beyond measure, doggedly pursued, and his long legs lessened at each jump the distance between. From a spectacular viewpoint, it must have been a pretty race.

The herder, with a gasp, dove into the tent; into the tent Happy Jack dove after him—and none too soon. The hand of the herder had almost clasped his rifle when the weight of Happy bore him shrieking to the earthen floor.

"Aw, yuh locoed old fool, shut up, can't yuh, a minute?" Happy Jack, with his fingers pressed against the windpipe of the other, had the satisfaction of seeing his request granted at once. The shrieks died to mere gurgling. "What I want uh *you*," Happy went on crossly, "ain't your lifeblood, yuh dam' Swede idiot. I want some clothes, and some grub; and I want to borry that pinto I seen picketed out in the hollow, down there. Now, will yuh let up that yelling and act white, or must I pound some p'liteness into yuh? Say!"

"By damn, Ay tank yo' vas got soom crazy," apologized the herder humbly, sanity growing in his pale blue eyes. "Ay tank—"

"Oh, I don't give a cuss what you *tank*," Happy Jack cut in. "I ain't had anything to eat sence yesterday forenoon, and I ain't had any clothes on sence yesterday, either. Send them darn dogs back to watch your sheep, and get busy with breakfast! I've got a lot to do, t'-day. I've got to round up my horse and get my clothes that's tied to the saddle, and get t' where I'm going. Get up, darn yuh! I ain't going t' eat yuh—not unless you're too slow with that grub."

The herder was submissive and placating, and permitted Happy Jack to appropriate the conventional garb of a male human, the while coffee and bacon were maddening his hunger with their tantalizing odor. He seemed much more at ease, once he saw that Happy Jack, properly clothed, was not particularly fearsome to look upon, and talked volubly while he got out bread and stewed prunes and boiled beans for the thrice-unexpected guest.

Happy Jack, clothed and fed, became himself again and prophesied gloomily: "The chances is, that horse uh mine'll be forty miles away and still going, by this time; but soon as I can round him up, I'll bring your pinto back. Yuh needn't t' worry none; I guess I got all the sense I've ever had."

Once more astride a horse—albeit the pinto pony of a sheepherder—Happy Jack felt abundantly able to cope with the situation. He made a detour that put him far from where the three he most dreaded to meet were apt to be, and struck out at the pinto's best pace for the river at the point where he had crossed so disastrously the day before.

Having a good memory for directions and localities, he easily found the place of unhappy memory; and taking up Stranger's trail through the sand from there, he got the general direction of his flight and followed vengefully after; rode for an hour up a long, grassy coulee, and came suddenly upon the fugitive feeding quietly beside a spring. The bundle of clothing was still tied firmly to the saddle, and at sight of it the face of Happy Jack relaxed somewhat from its gloom.

When Happy rode up and cast a loop over his head Stranger nickered a bit, as if he did not much enjoy freedom while he yet bore the trappings of servitude. And his submission was so instant and voluntary that Happy Jack had not the heart to do as he had threatened many times in the last few hours—"to beat the hide off him." Instead, he got hastily into his clothes—quite as if he feared they might again be whisked away from him—and then rubbed forgivingly the nose of Stranger, and solicitously pulled a few strands of his forelock from under the brow-band. In the heart of Happy Jack was a great peace, marred only by the physical discomforts of much sun-blister and many deep scratches. After that he got thankfully into his own saddle and rode gladly away, leading the pinto pony behind him. He had got out of the scrape, and the Happy Family would never find it out; it was not likely that they would chance upon the Swede herder, or if they did, that they would exchange with him many words. The Happy Family held itself physically, mentally, morally and socially far above sheepherders—and in that lay the safety of Happy Jack.

It was nearly noon when he reached again the sheep camp, and the Swede hospitably urged him to stay and eat with him; but Happy Jack would not tarry, for he was anxious to reach the camp of the Flying U. A mile from the herder's camp he saw again on a distant hilltop three familiar figures. This time he did not dodge into shelter, but urged Stranger to a gallop and rode boldly toward them. They greeted him joyfully and at the top of their voices when he came within shouting distance.

"How comes it you're riding the pinnacles over here?" Weary wanted to know, as soon as he rode alongside.

"Aw, I just came over after more orders; hope they send somebody else over there, if they want any more repping done," Happy Jack said, in his customary tone of discontent with circumstances.

"Say! Yuh didn't see anything of a wild man, down next the river, did yuh?" put in Pink.

"Aw, gwan! what wild man?" Happy Jack eyed them suspiciously.

"Honest, there's a wild man ranging around here in these hills," Pink declared. "We've been mooching around all forenoon, hunting him. Got sight of him, early this morning, but he got away in the brush."

Happy Jack looked guilty, and even more suspicious. Was it possible that they had recognized him?

"The way we come to hear about him," Weary explained, "we happened across some campers, over in a little coulee to the west uh here. They was all worked up over him. Seems he went into camp last night, and like to scared the ladies into fits. He ain't got enough clothes on to flag an antelope, according to them, and he's about seven feet high, and looks more like a missing link than a plain, ordinary man. The one that didn't faint away got the best look at him, and she's ready to take oath he ain't more'n half human. They kept fires burning all night to scare him out uh the coulee, and they're going to break camp to-day and hike for home. They say he give a screech that'd put a crimp in the devil himself, and went galloping off, jumping about twenty feet at a lick. And—"

"Aw, gwan!" protested Happy Jack, feebly.

"So help me Josephine, it's the truth," abetted Pink, round-eyed and unmistakably in earnest. "We wouldn't uh taken much stock in it, either, only we saw him ourselves, not more than two hundred yards off. He was just over the hill from the coulee where they were camped, so it's bound to be the same animal. It's a fact, he didn't have much covering—just something hung over his shoulders. And he was sure wild, for soon as he seen us he humped himself and got into the brush. We could hear him go crashing away like a whole bunch of elephants. It's a damn' shame he got away on us," Pink sighed regretfully. "We was going to rope him and put him in a cage; we could sure uh made money on him, at two bits a look."

Happy Jack continued to eye the three distrustfully. Too often had he been the victim of their humor for him now to believe implicitly in their ignorance. It was too good to be real, it seemed to him. Still, if by any good luck it *were* real, he hated to think what would happen if they ever found out the truth. He eased the clothing cautiously away from his smarting back, and stared hard into a coulee.

"It was likely some sheepherder gone clean nutty," mused Irish.

"Well, the most uh them wouldn't have far to go," ventured Happy Jack, thinking of the Swede.

"What we ought to do," said Pink, keen for the chase, "is for the whole bunch of us to come down here and round him up. Wonder if we couldn't talk Chip into laying off for a day or so; there's no herd to hold. I sure would like to get a good look at him."

"Somebody ought to take him in," observed Irish longingly. "He ain't safe, running around loose like that. There's no telling what he might do. The way them campers read his brand, he's plumb dangerous to meet up with alone. It's lucky you didn't run onto him, Happy."

"Well, I didn't," growled Happy Jack. "And what's more, I betche there ain't any such person."

"Don't call us liars to our faces, Happy," Weary reproved. "We told yuh, a dozen times, that we saw him ourselves. Yuh might be polite enough to take our word for it."

"Aw, gwan!" Happy Jack grunted, still not quite sure of how much—or how little—they knew. While they discussed further the wild man, he watched furtively for the surreptitious lowering of lids that would betray their insincerity. When they appealed to him for an opinion of some phase of the subject, he answered with caution. He tried to turn the talk to his experiences on the Shonkin range, and found the wild man cropping up with disheartening persistency. He shifted often in the saddle, because of the deep sunburns which smarted continually and maddeningly. He wondered if the boys had used all of that big box of carbolic salve which used to be kept in a corner of the mess-box; and was carbolic salve good for sun-blisters? He told himself gloomily that if there was any of it left, and if it were good for his ailment, there wouldn't be half enough of it, anyway. He estimated unhappily that he would need about two quarts.

When they reached camp, the welcome of Happy Jack was overshadowed and made insignificant by the strange story of the wild man. Happy Jack, mentally and physically miserable, was forced to hear it all told over again, and to listen to the excited comments of the others. He was sick of the subject. He had heard enough about the wild man, and he wished fervently that they would shut up about it. He couldn't see that it was anything to make such a fuss about, anyway. And he wished he could get his hands on that carbolic salve, without having the whole bunch rubbering around and asking questions about something that was none of their business. He even wished, in that first bitter hour after he had eaten and while they were lying idly in the shady spots, that he was back on the Shonkin range with an alien crew.

It was perhaps an hour later that Pink, always of an investigative turn of mind, came slipping quietly up through the rose bushes from the creek. The Happy Family, lying luxuriously upon the grass, were still discussing the latest excitement. Pink watched his chance and when none but Weary observed him jerked his head mysteriously toward the creek.

Weary got up, yawned ostentatiously, and sauntered away in the wake of Pink. "What's the matter, Cadwolloper?" he asked, when he was close enough. "Seen a garter snake?" Pink was notoriously afraid of snakes.

"You come with me, and I'll show yuh the wild man," he grinned.

"Mama!" ejaculated Weary, and followed stealthily where Pink led.

Some distance up the creek Pink signalled caution, and they crept like Indians on hands and knees through the grass. On the edge of the high bank they stopped, and Pink motioned. Weary looked over and came near whooping at the sight below. He gazed a minute, drew back and put his face close to the face of Pink.

"Cadwolloper, go get the bunch!" he commanded in a whisper, and Pink, again signalling needlessly for silence, slipped hastily away from the spot.

Happy Jack, secure in the seclusion offered by the high bank of the creek, ran his finger regretfully around the inside of the carbolic salve box, eyed the result dissatisfiedly, and applied the finger carefully to a deep cut on his knee. He had got that cut while going up the bluff, just after leaving the tent where had been the shrieking females. He wished there was more salve, and he picked up the cover of the box and painstakingly wiped out the inside; the result was disheartening.

He examined his knee dolefully. It was beginning to look inflamed, and it was going to make him limp. He wondered if the boys would notice anything queer about his walk. If they did, there was the conventional excuse that his horse had fallen down with him—Happy Jack hoped that it would be convincing. He took up the box again and looked at the shining emptiness of it. It had been half full—not enough, by a long way—and maybe some one would wonder what had become of it. Darn a bunch that always had to know everything, anyway!

Happy Jack, warned at last by that unnamed instinct which tells of a presence unseen, turned around and looked up apprehensively. The Happy Family, sitting in a row upon their heels on the bank, looked down at him gravely and appreciatively.

"There's a can uh wagon dope, up at camp," Cal Emmett informed him sympathetically.

"Aw—" Happy Jack began, and choked upon his humiliation.

"I used to know a piece uh poetry about a fellow like Happy," Weary remarked sweetly. "It said

> 'He raised his veil, the maid turned slowly round
> Looked at him, shrieked, and fell upon the ground.'

Only, in this case," Weary smiled blandly down upon him, "Happy didn't have no veil."

"Aw, gwan!" adjured Happy Jack helplessly, and reached for his clothes, while the Happy Family chorused a demand for explanations.

A TAMER OF WILD ONES.

When the days grow crisp at each end and languorous in the middle; when a haze ripples the skyline like a waving ribbon of faded blue; when the winds and the grasses stop and listen for the first on-rush of winter, then it is that the rangeland takes on a certain intoxicating unreality, and range-wild blood leaps with desire to do something—anything, so it is different and irresponsible and not measured by precedent or prudence.

In days like that one grows venturesome and ignores difficulties and limitations with a fine disregard for probable consequences, a mental snapping of fingers. On a day like that, the Happy Family, riding together out of Dry Lake with the latest news in mind and speech, urged Andy Green, tamer of wild ones, to enter the rough-riding contest exploited as one of the features of the Northern Montana Fair, to be held at Great Falls in two weeks. Pink could not enter, because a horse had fallen with him and hurt his leg, so that he was picking the gentlest in his string for daily riding. Weary would not, because he had promised his Little Schoolma'am to take care of himself and not take any useless risks; even the temptation of a two-hundred-dollar purse could not persuade him that a rough-riding contest is perfectly safe and without the ban. But Andy, impelled by the leaping blood of him and urged by the loyal Family, consented and said he'd try it a whirl, anyway.

They had only ridden four or five miles when the decision was reached, and they straightway turned back and raced into Dry Lake again, so that Andy might write the letter that clinched matters. Then, whooping with the sheer exhilaration of living, and the exultation of being able to ride and whoop unhindered, they galloped back to camp and let the news spread as it would. In a week all Chouteau County knew that Andy Green would ride for the purse, and nearly all Chouteau County backed him with all the money it could command; certainly, all of it that knew Andy Green and had seen him ride, made haste to find someone who did not know him and whose faith in another contestant was strong, and to bet all the money it could lay hands upon.

For Andy was one of those mild-mannered men whose genius runs to riding horses which object violently to being ridden; one of those lucky fellows who never seems to get his neck broken, however much he may jeopardize it; and, moreover, he was that rare genius, who can make a "pretty" ride where other broncho-fighters resemble nothing so much as a scarecrow in a cyclone. Andy not only could ride—he could ride gracefully. And the reason for that, not many knew: Andy, in the years before he wandered to the range, had danced, in spangled tights, upon the broad rump of a big gray horse which galloped around a saw-dust ring with the regularity of movement that suggested a machine, while a sober-clothed man in the center cracked a whip and yelped commands. Andy had jumped through blazing hoops and over sagging bunting while he rode—and he was just a trifle ashamed of the fact. Also—though it does not particularly matter—he had, later in the performance, gone hurtling around the big tent dressed in the garb of an ancient Roman and driving four deep-chested bays abreast. As has been explained, he never boasted of his circus experience; though his days in spangled tights probably had much to do with the inimitable grace of him in the saddle. The Happy Family felt to a man that Andy would win the purse and add honor to the Flying U in the winning. They were enthusiastic over the prospect and willing to bet all they had on the outcome.

The Happy Family, together with the aliens who swelled the crew to round-up size, was foregathered at the largest Flying U corral, watching a bunch of newly bought horses circle, with much snorting and kicking up of dust, inside the fence. It was the interval between beef-and calf-roundups, and the witchery of Indian Summer held the range-land in thrall.

Andy, sizing up the bunch and the brands, lighted upon a rangy blue roan that he knew—or thought he knew, and the eyes of him brightened with desire. If he could get that roan in his string, he told himself, he could go to sleep in the saddle on night-guard; for an easier horse to ride he never had straddled. It was like sitting in grandma's pet rocking chair when that roan loosened his muscles for a long, tireless gallop over the prairie sod, and as a stayer Andy had never seen his equal. It was not his turn to choose, however, and he held his breath lest the rope of another should settle over the slatey-black ears ahead of him.

Cal Emmett roped a plump little black and led him out, grinning satisfaction; from the white saddle-marks back of the withers he knew him for a "broke" horse, and he certainly was pretty to look at. Andy gave him but a fleeting glance.

Happy Jack spread his loop and climbed down from the fence, almost at Andy's elbow. It was his turn to choose. "I betche that there blue roan over there is a good one," he remarked. "I'm going to tackle him."

Andy took his cigarette from between his lips. "Yuh better hobble your stirrups, then," he discouraged artfully. "I know that roan a heap better than you do."

"Aw, gwan!" Happy, nevertheless, hesitated. "He's got a kind eye in his head; yuh can always go by a horse's eye."

"Can yuh?" Andy smiled indifferently. "Go after him, then. And say, Happy: if yuh ride that blue roan for five successive minutes, I'll give yuh fifty dollars. I knew that hoss down on the Musselshell; he's got a record that'd reach from here to Dry Lake and back." It was a bluff, pure and simple, born of his covetousness, but it had the desired effect—or nearly so.

Happy fumbled his rope and eyed the roan. "Aw, I betche you're just lying," he hazarded; but, like many another, when he did strike the truth he failed to recognize it. "I betche—"

"All right, rope him out and climb on, if yuh don't believe me." The tone of Andy was tinged with injury. "There's fifty dollars—yes, by gracious, I'll give yuh a *hundred* dollars if yuh ride him for five minutes straight."

A conversation of that character, carried on near the top of two full-lunged voices, never fails in the range land to bring an audience of every male human within hearing. All other conversations and interests were immediately suspended, and a dozen men trotted up to see what it was all about. Andy remained roosting upon the top rail, his rope coiled loosely and dangling from one arm while he smoked imperturbably.

"Oh, Happy was going to rope out a sure-enough bad one for his night hoss, and out uh the goodness uh my heart, I put him wise to what he was going up against," he explained carelessly.

"He acts like he has some thoughts uh doubting my word, so I just offered him a hundred dollars to ride him—that blue roan, over there next that crooked post. GET *a reserved seat right in front of the grand stand where all the big acts take* PLACE;" he sung out suddenly, in the regulation circus tone. "GET-a-seat-right-in-front-where-Happy-Jack-the-WILD-Man-rides-the-BUCKING-BRONCHO—Go on, Happy. Don't keep the audience waiting. Aren't yuh going to earn that hundred dollars?"

Happy Jack turned half a shade redder than was natural. "Aw, gwan. I never said I was going to do no broncho-busting ack. But I betche yuh never seen that roan before he was unloaded in Dry Lake."

"What'll yuh bet I don't know that hoss from a yearling colt?" Andy challenged, and Happy Jack walked away without replying, and cast his loop sullenly over the first horse he came to—which was *not* the roan.

Chip, coming up to hear the last of it, turned and looked long at the horse in question; a mild-mannered horse, standing by a crooked corral post and flicking his ears at the flies. "Do you know that roan?"he asked Andy, in the tone which brings truthful answer. Andy had one good point: he never lied except in an irresponsible mood of pure deviltry. For instance, he never had lied seriously, to an employer.

"Sure, I know that hoss," he answered truthfully.

"Did you ever ride him?"

"No," Andy admitted, still truthfully. "I never rode him but once myself, but I worked right with a Lazy 6 rep that had him in his string, down at the U up-and-down, two years ago. I know the hoss, all right; but I did lie when I told Happy I knowed him from a colt. I spread it on a little bit thick, there." He smiled engagingly down at Chip.

"And he's a bad one, is he?" Chip queried Over his shoulder, just as he was about to walk away.

"Well," Andy prevaricated—still clinging to the letter, if not to the spirit of truth. "He ain't a hoss I'd like to see Happy Jack go up against. I ain't saying, though, that he can't be *rode*. I don't say that about *any* hoss."

"Is he any worse than Glory, when Glory is feeling peevish?" Weary asked, when Chip was gone and while the men still lingered. Andy, glancing to make sure that Chip was out of hearing, threw away his cigarette and yielded to temptation. "Glory?" he snorted with a fine contempt. "Why, Glory's—a—*lamb* beside that blue roan! Why, that hoss throwed Buckskin Jimmy clean out of a corral—Did yuh ever see Buckskin Jimmy ride? Well, say, yuh missed a pretty sight, then; Jimmy's a sure-enough rider. About the only animal he ever failed to connect with for keeps, is that same cow-backed hoss yuh see over there. Happy says he's got a kind eye in his head—" Andy stopped and laughed till they all laughed with him. "By gracious, Happy ought to step up *on* him, once, and see how *kind* he is!" He laughed again until Happy, across the corral saddling the horse he had chosen, muttered profanely at the derision he knew was pointed at himself.

"Why, I've seen that hoss—" Andy Green, once fairly started in the fascinating path of romance, invented details for the pure joy of creation. If he had written some of the tales he told, and had sold the writing for many dollars, he would have been famous. Since he did not write them for profit, but told them for fun, instead, he earned merely the reputation of being a great liar. A significant mark of his genius lay in the fact that his inventions never failed to convince; not till afterward did his audience doubt.

That is why the blue roan was not chosen in any of the strings, but was left always circling in the corral after a loop had settled. That is why the Flying U boys looked at him askance as they passed him by. That is why, when a certain Mr. Coleman, sent by the board of directors to rake northern Montana for bad horses, looked with favor upon the blue roan when he came to the Flying U ranch and heard the tale of his exploits as interpreted—I should say created—by Andy Green.

"We've got to have him," he declared enthusiastically. "If he's as bad as all that, he'll be the star performer at the contest, and make that two-hundred-dollar plum a hard one to pick. Some of these gay boys have entered with the erroneous idea that that same plum is hanging loose, and all they've got to do is lean up against the tree and it'll drop in their mouths. We've got to have that roan. I'll pay you a good price for him, Whitmore, if you won't let him go any other way. We've got a reporter up there that can do him up brown in a special article, and people will come in bunches to see a horse with that kind of a pedigree. Is it Green, here, that knows the horse and what he'll do? You're sure of him, are you, Green?"

Andy took time to roll a cigarette. He had not expected any such development as this, and he needed to think of the best way out. All he had wanted or intended was to discourage the others from claiming the blue roan; he wanted him in his own string. Afterwards, when they had pestered him about the roan's record, he admitted to himself that he had, maybe, overshot the mark and told it a bit too scarey, and too convincingly. Under the spell of fancy he had done more than make the roan unpopular as a roundup horse; he had made him a celebrity in the way of outlaw horses. And they wanted him in the rough-riding contest! Andy, perhaps, had never before been placed in just such a position.

"Are you sure of what the horse will do?" Mr. Coleman repeated, seeing that Andy was taking a long time to reply.

Andy licked his cigarette, twisted an end and leaned backward while he felt in his pocket for a match. From the look of his face you never could have told how very uncomfortable he felt "Naw," he drawled. "I ain't never sure of what *any* hoss will do. I've had too much dealings with 'em for any uh that brand uh foolishness." He lighted the cigarette as if that were the only matter in which he took any real interest, though he was thinking fast.

Mr. Coleman looked nonplussed. "But I thought—you said—"

"What I said," Andy retorted evenly, "hit the blue roan two years ago; maybe he's reformed since then; I dunno. Nobody's rode him, here." He could not resist a sidelong glance at Happy Jack. "There was some talk of it, but it never come to a head."

"Yuh offered me a hundred dollars—" Happy Jack began accusingly.

"And yuh never made no move to earn it, that I know of. By gracious, yuh all seem to think I ought to *mind*-read that hoss! I ain't seen him for two years. Maybe so, he's a real wolf yet; maybe so, he's a sheep." He threw out both his hands to point the end of the argument—so far as he was concerned—stuck them deep into his trousers' pockets and walked away before he could be betrayed into deeper deceit. It did seem to him rather hard that, merely because he had wanted the roan badly enough to—er—exercise a little diplomacy in order to get him, they should keep harping on the subject like that. And to have Coleman making medicine to get the roan into that contest was, to say the least, sickening. Andy's private belief was that a twelve-year-old girl could go round up the milk-cows on that horse. He had never known him to make a crooked move, and he had ridden beside him all one summer and had seen him in all places and under all possible conditions. He was a dandy cow-horse, and dead gentle; all this talk made him tired. Andy had forgotten that he himself had started the talk.

Coleman went often to the corral when the horses were in, and looked at the blue roan. Later he rode on to other ranches where he had heard were bad horses, and left the roan for further consideration. When he was gone, Andy breathed freer and put his mind to the coming contest and the things he meant to do with the purse and with the other contestants.

"That Diamond G twister is going t' ride," Happy Jack announced, one day when he came from town. "Some uh the boys was in town and they said so. He can ride, too. I betche Andy don't have no picnic gitting the purse away from *that* feller. And Coleman's got that sorrel outlaw uh the HS. I betche Andy'll have to pull leather on that one." This was, of course, treason pure and simple; but Happy Jack's prophecies were never taken seriously.

Andy simply grinned at him. "Put your money on the Diamond G twister," he advised calmly. "I know him—he's a good rider, too. His name's Billy Roberts. Uh course, I aim to beat him to it, but Happy never does like to have a sure-thing. He wants something to hang his jaw down over. Put your money on Billy and watch it fade away, Happy."

"Aw, gwan. I betche that there sorrel—"

"I rode that there sorrel once, and combed his forelock with both spurs alternate," Andy lied boldly. "He's pickings. Take him back and bring me a real hoss."

Happy Jack wavered. "Well, I betche yuh don't pull down that money," he predicted vaguely. "I betche yuh git throwed, or something. It don't do to be too blame sure uh nothing."

Whereat Andy laughed derisively and went away whistling. "I wish I was as sure uh living till I was a thousand years old, and able to ride nine months out of every year of 'em," he called back to Happy. Then he took up the tune where he had left off.

For the days were still crisp at both ends and languorous in the middle, and wind and grasses hushed and listened for the coming of winter. And because of these things, and his youth and his health, the heart of Andy Green was light in his chest and trouble stood afar off with its face turned from him.

It was but three days to the opening of the fair when Coleman, returning that way from his search for bad horses, clattered, with his gleanings and three or four men to help drive them, down the grade to the Flying U. And in the Flying U coulee, just across the creek from the corrals, still rested the roundup tents for a space. For the shipping was over early and work was not urgent, and Chip and the Old Man, in their enthusiasm for the rough-riding contest and the entry of their own man, had decided to take the wagons and crew entire to Great Falls and camp throughout the four days of the fair. The boys all wanted to go, anyway, as did everybody else, so that nothing could be done till it was over. It was a novel idea, and it tickled the humor of the Happy Family.

The "rough string," as the bad horses were called, was corralled, and the men made merry with the roundup crew. Diamond G men they were, loudly proclaiming their faith in Billy Roberts, and offering bets already against Andy, who listened undisturbed and had very little to say. The Happy Family had faith in him, and that was enough. If everybody, he told them, believed that he would win, where would be the fun of riding and showing them?

It was after their early supper that Coleman came down to camp at the heels of Chip and the Old Man. Straightway he sought out Andy like a man who has something on his mind; though Andy did not in the least know what it was, he recognized the indefinable symptoms and braced himself mentally, half suspecting that it was something about that blue roan again. He was getting a little bit tired of the blue roan—enough so that, though he had chosen him for his string, he had not yet put saddle to his back, but waited until the roundup started out once more, when he would ride him in his turn.

It was the blue roan, without doubt. Coleman came to a stop directly in front of Andy, and as directly came to the point.

"Look here, Green," he began. "I'm shy on horses for that contest, and Whitmore and Bennett say I can have that roan you've got in your string. If he's as bad as you claim, I certainly must have him. But you seem to have some doubts of what he'll do, and I'd like to see him ridden once. Your shingle is out as a broncho-peeler. Will you ride him this evening, so I can size him up for that contest?"

Andy glanced up under his eyebrows, and then sidelong at the crowd. Every man within hearing was paying strict attention, and was eyeing him expectantly; for broncho-fighting is a spectacle that never palls.

"Well, I can ride him, if yuh say so," Andy made cautious answer, "but I won't gamble he's a bad hoss *now*—that is, bad enough to take to the Falls. Yuh don't want to expect—"

"Oh, I don't expect anything—only I want to see him ridden once. Come on, no time like the present. If he's bad, you'll have to ride him at the fair, anyhow, and a little practice won't hurt you; and if he isn't, I want to know it for sure."

"It's a go with me," Andy said indifferently, though he secretly felt much relief. The roan would go off like a pet dog, and he could pretend to be somewhat surprised, and declare that he had reformed. Bad horses do reform, sometimes, as Andy and every other man in the crowd knew. Then there would be no more foolish speculation about the cayuse, and Andy could keep him in peace and have a mighty good cow-pony, as he had schemed. He smoked a cigarette while Chip was having the horses corralled, and then led the way willingly, with twenty-five men following expectantly at his heels. Unlike Andy, they fully expected an impromptu exhibition of fancy riding. Not all of them had seen Andy atop a bad horse, and the Diamond G men, in particular, were eager to witness a sample of his skill.

The blue roan submitted to the rope, and there was nothing spectacular in the saddling. Andy kept his cigarette between his lips and smiled to himself when he saw the saddle bunch hazed out through the gate and the big corral left empty of every animal but the blue roan, as was customary when a man tackled a horse with the record which he had given the poor beast. Also, the sight of twenty-five men roosting high, their boot-heels hooked under a corral rail to steady them, their faces writ large with expectancy, amused him inwardly. He pictured their disappointment when the roan trotted around the corral once or twice at his bidding, and smiled again.

"If you can't top him, Green, we'll send for Billy Roberts. *He'll* take off the rough edge and gentle him down for yuh," taunted a Diamond G man.

"Don't get excited till the show starts," Andy advised, holding the cigarette in his fingers while he emptied his lungs of smoke. Just to make a pretence of caution, he shook the saddle tentatively by the horn, and wished the roan would make a little show of resistance, instead of standing there like an old cow, lacking only the cud, as he complained to himself, to make the resemblance complete. The roan, however, did lay back an ear when Andy, the cigarette again in his lips, put his toe in the stirrup.

"Go after it, you weatherbeaten old saw-buck," he yelled, just to make the play strong, before he was fairly in the saddle.

Then it was that the Happy Family, heart and soul and pocket all for Andy Green and his wonderful skill in the saddle; with many dollars backing their belief in him and with voices ever ready to sing his praises; with the golden light of early sunset all about them and the tang of coming night-frost in the air, received a shock that made them turn white under their tan.

"Mama!" breathed Weary, in a horrified half-whisper.

And Slim, goggle-eyed beside him, blurted, "Well, by *golly!*" in a voice that carried across the corral.

For Andy Green, tamer of wild ones (forsooth!) broncho-twister with a fame that not the boundary of Chouteau County held, nor yet the counties beyond; Andy Green, erstwhile "André de Gréno, champion bare-back rider of the Western Hemisphere," who had jumped through blazing hoops and over sagging bunting while he rode, turned handsprings and done other public-drawing feats, was prosaically, unequivocally "piled" at the fifth jump!

That he landed lightly on his feet, with the cigarette still between his lips, the roosting twenty-five quite overlooked. They saw only the first jump, where Andy, riding loose and unguardedly, went up on the blue withers. The second, third and fourth jumps were not far enough apart to be seen and judged separately; as well may one hope to decide whether a whirling wheel had straight or crooked spokes. The fifth jump, however, was a masterpiece of rapid-fire contortion, and it was important because it left Andy on the ground, gazing, with an extremely grieved expression, at the uninterrupted convolutions of the "dandy little cow-hoss."

The blue roan never stopped so much as to look back. He was busy—exceedingly busy. He was one of those perverted brutes which buck and bawl and so keep themselves wrought up to a high pitch—literally and figuratively. He set himself seriously to throw Andy's saddle over his head, and he was not a horse which easily accepts defeat. Andy walked around in the middle of the corral, quite aimlessly, and watched the roan contort. He could not understand in the least, and his amazement overshadowed, for the moment, the fact that he had been thrown and that in public and before men of the Diamond G.

Then it was that the men of the Diamond G yelled shrill words of ironical sympathy. Then it was that the Happy Family looked at one another in shamed silence, and to the taunts of the Diamond Gs made no reply. It had never occurred to them that such a thing could happen. Had they not seen Andy ride, easily and often? Had they not heard from Pink how Andy had performed that difficult feat at the Rocking R—the feat of throwing his horse flat in the middle of a jump? They waited until the roan, leaving the big corral looking, in the fast deepening twilight, like a fresh-ploughed field, stopped dejectedly and stood with his nose against the closed gate, and then climbed slowly down from the top rail of the corral, still silent with the silence more eloquent than speech in any known language.

Over by the gate, Andy was yanking savagely at the latigo; and he, also, had never a word to say. He was still wondering how it had happened. He looked the roan over critically and shook his head against the riddle; for he had known him to be a quiet, dependable, all-round good horse, with no bad traits and an easy-going disposition that fretted at nothing. A high-strung, nervous beast might, from rough usage and abuse, go "bad"; but the blue roan—they had called him Pardner—had never showed the slightest symptom of nerves. Andy knew horses as he knew himself. That a horse like Pardner should, in two years, become an evil-tempered past-master in such devilish pitching as that, was past belief.

"I guess he'll do, all right," spoke Coleman at his elbow. "I've seen horses pitch, and I will say that he's got some specialties that are worth exhibiting." Then, as a polite way of letting Andy down easy, he added, "I don't wonder you couldn't connect."

"Connect—*hell*!" It was Andy's first realization of what his failure meant to the others. He left off wondering about the roan, and faced the fact that he had been thrown, fair and square, and that before an audience of twenty-five pairs of eyes which had seen rough riding before, and which had expected of him something better than they were accustomed to seeing.

"I reckon Billy Roberts will have to work on that cayuse a while," fleered a Diamond G man, coming over to them. "He'll gentle him down so that anybody— *even Green*, can ride him!"

Andy faced him hotly, opened his mouth for sharp reply, and closed it. He had been "piled." Nothing that he could say might alter that fact, nor explanations lighten the disgrace. He turned and went out the gate, carrying his saddle and bridle with him.

"Aw—and you was goin' t' ride in that contest!" wailed Happy Jack recriminatingly. "And I've got forty dollars up on yuh!"

"Shut up!" snapped Pink in his ear, heart-broken but loyal to the last. "Yuh going to blat around and let them Diamond Gs give yuh the laugh? Hunt up something you can use for a backbone till they get out uh camp, for Heaven's sake! Andy's our man. So help me, Josephine, if anybody goes rubbing it in where I can hear, he'll get his face punched!"

"Say, I guess we ain't let down on our faces, or anything!" sighed Cal Emmett, coming up to them. "I thought Andy could ride! Gee whiz, but it was fierce! Why, *Happy* could make a better ride than that!"

"By golly, I want t' have a talk with that there broncho-tamer," Slim growled behind them. "I got money on him. Is he goin t' ride for that purse? 'Cause if he is, I ain't going a foot."

These and other remarks of a like nature made up the clamor that surged in the ears of Andy as he went, disgraced and alone, up to the deserted bunk-house where he need not hear what they were saying. He knew, deep in his heart, that he could ride that horse. He had been thrown because of his own unpardonable carelessness—a carelessness which he could not well explain to the others. He himself had given the roan an evil reputation; a reputation that, so far as he knew, was libel pure and simple. To explain now that he was thrown simply because he never dreamed the horse would pitch, and so was taken unaware, would simply be to insult their intelligence. He was not supposed, after mounting a horse like that, to be taken unaware. He might, of course, say that he had lied all along—but he had no intention of making any confession like that. Even if he did, they would not believe him. Altogether, it was a very unhappy young man who slammed his spurs into a far corner and kicked viciously a box he had stumbled over in the dusk.

"Trying to bust the furniture?" it was the voice of the Old Man at the door.

"By gracious, it seems I can't bust *bronks* no more," Andy made rueful reply. "I reckon I'll just about have to bust the furniture or nothing."

The Old Man chuckled and came inside, sought the box Andy had kicked, and sat down upon it. Through the open door came the jumble of many voices upraised in fruitless argument, and with it the chill of frost. The Old Man fumbled for his pipe, filled it and scratched a match sharply on the box. In the flare of it Andy watched his kind old face with its fringe of grayish hair and its deep-graven lines of whimsical humor.

"Doggone them boys, they ain't got the stayin' qualities I give 'em credit for having," he remarked, holding up the match and looking across at Andy, humped disconsolately in the shadows. "Them Diamond G men has just about got 'em on the run, right now. Yuh couldn't get a hundred-t'-one bet, down there."

Andy merely grunted.

"Say," asked the Old Man suddenly. "Didn't yuh kinda mistake that blue roan for his twin brother, Pardner? This here cayuse is called Weaver. I tried t' get hold of t'other one, but doggone 'em, they wouldn't loosen up. Pardner wasn't for sale at no price, but they talked me into buying the Weaver; they claimed he's just about as good a horse, once he's tamed down some—and I thought, seein' I've got some real *tamers* on my pay-roll, I'd take a chance on him. I thought yuh knew the horse—the way yuh read up his pedigree—till I seen yuh mount him. Why, doggone it, yuh straddled him like yuh was just climbing a fence! Maybe yuh know your own business best—but didn't yuh kinda mistake him for Pardner? They're as near alike as two bullets run in the same mold—as far as *looks* go."

Andy got up and went to the door, and stood looking down the dusk-muffled hill to the white blotch which was the camp; listened to the jumble of voices still upraised in fruitless argument, and turned to the Old Man.

"By gracious, that accounts for a whole lot," he said ambiguously.

II

"I don't see," said Cal Emmett crossly, "what's the use uh this whole outfit trailing up to that contest. If I was Chip, I'd call the deal off and start gathering calves. It ain't as if we had a man to ride for that belt and purse. Ain't your leg well enough to tackle it, Pink?"

"No," Pink answered shortly, "it ain't."

"Riding the rough bunch they've rounded up for that contest ain't going to be any picnic," Weary defended his chum. "Cadwolloper would need two good legs to go up against that deal."

"I wish Irish was here," Pink gloomed. "I'd be willing to back him; all right. But it's too late now; he couldn't enter if he was here."

A voice behind them spoke challengingly. "I don't believe it would be etiquette for one outfit to enter *two* peelers. One's enough, ain't it?"

The Happy Family turned coldly upon the speaker. It was Slim who answered for them all. "I dunno as this outfit has got *any* peeler in that contest. By golly, it don't look like it since las' night!"

Weary was gentle, as always, but he was firm. "We kinda thought you'd want to withdraw," he added.

Andy Green, tamer of wild ones, turned and eyed Weary curiously. One might guess, from telltale eyes and mouth, that his calmness did not go very deep. "I don't recollect mentioning that I was busy penning any letter uh withdrawal," he said. "I got my sights raised to that purse and that belt. I don't recollect saying anything about lowering 'em."

"Aw, gwan. I guess *I'll* try for that purse, too! I betche I got as good a show as—"

"Sure. Help yourself, it don't cost nothing. I don't doubt but what you'd make a real pretty ride, Happy." Andy's tone was deceitfully hearty. He did not sound in the least as if he would like to choke Happy Jack, though that was his secret longing.

"Aw, gwan. I betche I could make as purty a ride as we've saw—lately." Happy Jack did not quite like to make the thing too personal, for fear of what might happen after.

"Yuh mean last night, don't yuh?" purred Andy.

"Well, by golly, I wish you'd tell us what yuh done it for!" Slim cut in disgustedly. "It was nacherlay supposed you could ride; we got *money* up on yuh! And then, by golly, to go and make a fluke like that before them Diamond G men—to go and let that blue roan pile yuh up b'fore he'd got rightly started t' pitch—If yuh'd stayed with him till he got t' swappin' ends there, it wouldn't uh looked quite so bad. But t' go and git throwed down right in the start—By golly!" Slim faced Andy accusingly. "B'fore them Diamond G men—and I've got money up, by golly!"

"Yuh ain't lost any money yet, have yuh?" Andy inquired patiently. What Andy felt like doing was to "wade into the bunch"; reason, however, told him that he had it coming from them, and to take his medicine, since he could not well explain just how it had happened. He could not in reason wonder that the faith of the Happy Family was shattered and that they mourned as lost the money they had already rashly wagered on the outcome of the contest. The very completeness of their faith in him, their very loyalty, seemed to them their undoing, for to them the case was plain enough. If Andy could not ride the blue roan in their own corral, how was he to ride that same blue roan in Great Falls? Or, if he could ride him, how could any sane man hope that he could win the purse and the belt under the stringent rules of the contest, where "riding on the spurs," "pulling leather" and a dozen other things were barred? So Andy, under the sting of their innuendoes and blunt reproaches, was so patient as to seem to them cowed.

"No, I ain't lost any yet, but by golly, I can see it fixin' to fly," Slim retorted heavily.

Andy looked around at the others, and smiled as sarcastically as was possible considering the mood he was in. "It sure does amuse me," he observed, "to see growed men cryin' before they're hurt! By gracious, I expect t' make a stake out uh that fall! I can get long odds from them Diamond Gs, and from anybody they get a chance to talk to. I'm kinda planning," he lied boldly, "to winter in an orange grove and listen at the birds singing, after I'm through with the deal."

"I reckon yuh can count on hearing the birds sing, all right," Pink snapped back. "It'll be *tra-la-la* for yours, if last night's a fair sample uh what yuh expect to do with the blue roan." Pink walked abruptly away, looking very much like a sulky cherub.

"I s'pose yuh're aiming to give us the impression that you're going to ride, just the same," said Cal Emmett.

"I sure am," came brief reply. Andy was beginning to lose his temper. He had expected that the Happy Family would "throw it into him," to a certain extent, and he had schooled himself to take their drubbing. What he had not expected was their unfriendly attitude, which went beyond mere disappointment and made his offence—if it could be called that—more serious than the occasion would seem to warrant. Perhaps Jack Bates unwittingly made plain the situation when he remarked:

"I hate to turn down one of our bunch; we've kinda got in the habit uh hanging together and backing each other's play, regardless. But darn it, we ain't millionaires, none of us—and gambling, it is a sin. I've got enough up already to keep me broke for six months if I lose, and the rest are in about the same fix. I ain't raising no long howl, Andy, but you can see yourself where we're kinda bashful about sinking any more on yuh than what we have. Maybe you can ride; I've heard yuh can, and I've seen yuh make some fair rides, myself. But yuh sure fell down hard last night, and my faith in yuh got a jolt that fair broke its back. If yuh done it deliberate, for reasons we don't know, for Heaven's sake say so, and we'll take your word for it and forget your rep for lying. On the dead, Andy, did yuh fall off deliberate?"

Andy bit his lip. His conscience had a theory of its own about truth-telling, and permitted him to make strange assertions at times. Still, there were limitations. The Happy Family was waiting for his answer, and he knew instinctively that they would believe him now. For a moment, temptation held him. Then he squared his shoulders and spoke truly.

"On the dead, I hit the ground unexpected and inadvertant. I—"

"If that's the case, then the farther yuh keep away from that contest the better—if yuh ask *me*." Jack turned on his heel and followed Pink.

Andy stared after him moodily, then glanced at the rest. With one accord they avoided meeting his gaze. "Damn a bunch uh quitters!" he flared hotly, and left them, to hunt up the Old Man and Chip—one or both, it did not matter to him.

Pink it was who observed the Old Man writing a check for Andy. He took it that Andy had called for his time, and when Andy rolled his bed and stowed it away in the bunk-house, saddled a horse and rode up the grade toward town, the whole outfit knew for a certainty that Andy had quit.

Before many hours had passed they, too, saddled and rode away, with the wagons and the cavvy following after—and they were headed for Great Falls and the fair there to be held; or, more particularly, the rough-riding contest to which they had looked forward eagerly and with much enthusiasm, and which they were now approaching gloomily and in deep humiliation. Truly, it would be hard to find a situation more galling to the pride of the Happy Family.

But Andy Green had not called for his time, and he had no intention of quitting; for Andy was also suffering from that uncomfortable malady which we call hurt pride, and for it he knew but one remedy—a remedy which he was impatient to apply. Because of the unfriendly attitude of the Happy Family, Andy had refused to take them into his confidence, or to ride with them to the fair. Instead, he had drawn what money was still placed to his credit on the pay-roll, had taken a horse and his riding outfit and gone away to Dry Lake, where he intended to take the train for Great Falls.

In Dry Lake, however, he found that the story of his downfall had preceded him, thanks to the exultant men of the Diamond G, and that the tale had not shrunk in the telling. Dry Lake jeered him as openly as it dared, and part of it— that part which had believed in him—was quite as unfriendly as was the Happy Family. To a man they took it for granted that he would withdraw from the contest, and they were not careful to conceal what they thought. Andy found himself rather left alone, and he experienced more than once the unpleasant sensation of having conversation suddenly lag when he came near, and of seeing groups of men dissolve awkwardly at his approach. Andy, before he had been in town an hour, was in a mood to do violence.

For that reason he kept his plans rigidly to himself. When someone asked him if he had quit the outfit, he had returned gruffly that the Flying U was not the only cow-outfit in the country, and let the questioner interpret it as he liked. When the train that had its nose pointed to the southwest slid into town, Andy did not step on, as had been his intention. He remained idly leaning over the bar in Rusty Brown's place, and gave no heed. Later, when the eastbound came schreeching through at midnight, it found Andy Green on the platform with his saddle, bridle, chaps, quirt and spurs neatly sacked, and with a ticket for Havre in his pocket. So the wise ones said that they knew Andy would never have the nerve to show up at the fair, after the fluke he had made at the Flying U ranch, and those whose pockets were not interested considered it a very good joke.

At Havre, Andy bought another ticket and checked the sack which held his riding outfit; the ticket had Great Falls printed on it in bold, black lettering. So that he was twelve hours late in reaching his original destination, and to avoid unwelcome discovery and comment he took the sleeper and immediately ordered his berth made up, that he might pass through Dry Lake behind the sheltering folds of the berth curtains. Not that there was need of this elaborate subterfuge. He was simply mad clear through and did not want to see or hear the voice of any man he knew. Besides, the days when he had danced in spangled tights upon the broad, gray rump of a galloping horse while a sober-clothed man in the middle of the ring cracked a whip and yelped commands, had bred in him the unconscious love of a spectacular entry and a dramatic finish.

That is why he sought out the most obscure rooming house that gave any promise of decency and comfort, and stayed off Central Avenue and away from its loitering groups of range dwellers who might know him. That is why he hired a horse and rode early and alone to the fair grounds on the opening day, and avoided, by a roundabout trail a certain splotch of gray-white against the brown of the prairie, which he knew instinctively to be the camp of the Flying U outfit, which had made good time and were located to their liking near the river. Andy felt a tightening of the chest when he saw the familiar tents, and kicked his hired horse ill-naturedly in the ribs. It was all so different from what he had thought it would be.

In those last two weeks, he had pictured himself riding vaingloriously through town on his best horse, with a new Navajo saddle-blanket making a dab of bright color, and a new Stetson hat dimpled picturesquely as to crown and tilted rakishly over one eye, and with his silver-mounted spurs catching the light; around him would ride the Happy Family, also in gala attire and mounted upon the best horses in their several strings. The horses would not approve of the street-cars, and would circle and back—and it was quite possible, even probable, that there would be some pitching and some pretty riding before the gaping populace which did not often get a chance to view the real thing. People would stop and gaze while they went clattering by, and he, Andy Green, would be pointed out by the knowing ones as a fellow that was going to ride in the contest and that stood a good chance of winning. For Andy was but human, that he dreamed of these things; besides, does not the jumping through blazing hoops and over sagging bunting while one rides, whet insiduously one's appetite for the plaudits of the crowd?

The reality was different. He was in Great Falls, but he had not ridden vaingloriously down Central Avenue surrounded by the Happy Family, and watched by the gaping populace. Instead, he had chosen a side street and he had ridden alone, and no one had seemed to know or care who he might be. His horse had not backed, wild-eyed, before an approaching car, and he had not done any pretty riding. Instead, his horse had scarce turned an eye toward the jangling bell when he crossed the track perilously close to the car, and he had gone "side-wheeling" decorously down the street—and Andy hated a pacing horse. The Happy Family was in town, but he did not know where. Andy kicked his horse into a gallop and swore bitterly that he did not care. He did not suppose that they gave him a thought, other than those impelled by their jeopardized pockets. And that, he assured himself pessimistically, is friendship!

He tied the hired horse to the fence and went away to the stables and fraternized with a hump-backed jockey who knew a few things himself about riding and was inclined to talk unprofessionally. It was not at all as Andy had pictured the opening day, but he got through the time somehow until the crowd gathered and the racing began. Then he showed himself in the crowd of "peelers" and their friends, as unconcernedly as he might; and as unobtrusively. The Happy Family, he observed, was not there, though he met Chip face to face and had a short talk with him. Chip was the only one, aside from the Old Man, who really understood. Billy Roberts was there, and he greeted Andy commiseratingly, as one speaks to the sick or to one in mourning; the tone made Andy grind his teeth, though he knew in his heart that Billy Roberts wished him well—up to the point of losing the contest to him, which was beyond human nature. Billy Roberts was a rider and knew—or thought he knew—just how "sore" Andy must be feeling. Also, in the kindness of his heart he tried blunderingly to hide his knowledge.

"Going up against the rough ones?" he queried with careful carelessness, in the hope of concealing that he had heard the tale of Andy's disgrace.

"I sure am," Andy returned laconically, with no attempt to conceal anything.

Billy Roberts opened his eyes wide, and his mouth a little before he recovered from his surprise. "Well, good luck to yuh," he managed to say, "only so yuh don't beat me to it. I was kinda hoping yuh was too bashful to get out and ride before all the ladies."

Andy, remembering his days in the sawdust ring, smiled queerly; but his heart warmed to Billy Roberts amazingly.

They were leaning elbows on the fence below the grand stand, watching desultorily the endless preparatory manoeuvres of three men astride the hind legs of three pacers in sulkies. "This side-wheeling business gives me a pain," Billy remarked, as the pacers ambled by for the fourth or fifth time. "I like *caballos* that don't take all day to wind 'em up before they go. I been looking over our bunch. They's horses in that corral that are sure going to do things to us twenty peelers!"

"By gracious, yes!" Andy was beginning to feel himself again. "That blue hoss—uh course yuh heard how he got me, and heard it with trimmings—yuh may think he's a man-eater; but while he's a bad hoss, all right, he ain't the one that'll get yuh. Yuh want t' watch out, Billy, for that HS sorrel. He's plumb wicked. He's got a habit uh throwing himself backwards. They're keeping it quiet, maybe—but I've seen him do it three times in one summer."

"All right—thanks. I didn't know that. But the blue roan—"

"The blue roan'll pitch and bawl and swap ends on yuh and raise hell all around, but he can be rode. That festive bunch up in the reserve seats'll think it's awful, and that the HS sorrel is a lady's hoss alongside him, but a real rider can wear him out. But that sorrel—when yuh think yuh got him beat, Billy, is when yuh want to watch out!"

Billy turned his face away from a rolling dustcloud that came down the home stretch with the pacers, and looked curiously at Andy. Twice he started to speak and did not finish. Then: "A man can be a sure-enough rider, and get careless and let a horse pile him off him when he ain't looking, just because he knows he can ride that horse," he said with a certain diffidence.

"By gracious, yes!" Andy assented emphatically. And that was the nearest they came to discussing a delicate matter which was in the minds of both.

Andy was growing more at ease and feeling more optimistic every minute. Three men still believed in him, which was much. Also, the crowd could not flurry him as it did some of the others who were not accustomed to so great an audience; rather, it acted as a tonic and brought back the poise, the easy self-confidence which had belonged to one André de Gréno, champion bareback rider. So that, when the rough-riding began, Andy's nerves were placidly asleep.

At the corral in the infield, where the horses and men were foregathered, Andy met Slim and Happy Jack; but beyond his curt "Hello" and an amazed "Well, by golly!" from Slim, no words passed. Across the corral he glimpsed some of the others—Pink and Weary, and farther along, Cal Emmett and Jack Bates; but they made no sign if they saw him, and he did not go near them. He did not know when his turn would come to ride, and he had a horse to saddle at the command of the powers that were. Coleman, the man who had collected the horses, almost ran over him. He said "Hello, Green," and passed on, for his haste was great.

Horse after horse was saddled and led perforce out into the open of the infield; man after man mounted, with more or less trouble, and rode to triumph or defeat. Billy Roberts was given a white-eyed little bay, and did some great riding. The shouts and applause from the grand stand rolled out to them in a great wave of sound. Billy mastered the brute and rode him back to the corral white-faced and with beads of sweat standing thick on his forehead.

"It ain't going to be such damn' easy money—that two hundred," he confided pantingly to Andy, who stood near. "The fellow that gets it will sure have to earn it."

Andy nodded and moved out where he could get a better view. Then Coleman came and informed him hurriedly that he came next, and Andy went back to his place. The horse he was to ride he had never seen before that day. He was a long-legged brown, with scanty mane and a wicked, rolling eye. He looked capable of almost any deviltry, but Andy did not give much time to speculating upon what he would try to do. He was still all eyes to the infield where his predecessor was gyrating. Then a sudden jump loosened him so that he grabbed the horn—and it was all over with that particular applicant, so far as the purse and the championship belt were concerned. He was out of the contest, and presently he was also back at the corral, explaining volubly—and uselessly—just how it came about. He appeared to have a very good reason for "pulling leather," but Andy was not listening and only thought absently that the fellow was a fool to make a talk for himself.

Andy was clutching the stirrup and watching a chance to put his toe into it, and the tall brown horse was circling backwards with occasional little side-jumps. When it was quite clear that the horse did not mean to be mounted, Andy reached out his hand, got a rope from somebody—he did not know who, though, as a matter of fact, it was Pink who gave it—and snared a front foot; presently the brown was standing upon three legs instead of four, and the gaping populace wondered how it was done, and craned necks to see. After that, though the horse still circled backwards, Andy got the stirrup and put his toe in it and went up so easily that the ignorant might think anybody could do it. He dropped the rope and saw that it was Pink who picked it up.

The brown at first did nothing at all. Then he gave a spring straight ahead and ran fifty yards or so, stopped and began to pitch. Three jumps and he ran again; stopped and reared. It was very pretty to look at, but Happy Jack could have ridden him, or Slim, or any other range rider. In two minutes the brown was sulking, and it took severe spurring to bring him back to the corral. Pitch he would not. The crowd applauded, but Andy felt cheated and looked as he felt.

Pink edged toward him, but Andy was not in the mood for reconciliation and kept out of his way. Others of the Happy Family came near, at divers times and places, as if they would have speech with him, but he thought he knew about what they would say, and so was careful not to give them a chance. When the excitement was all over for that day he got his despised hired horse and went back to town with Billy Roberts, because it was good to have a friend and because they wanted to talk about the riding. Billy did not tell Andy, either, that he had had hard work getting away from his own crowd; for Billy was kind-hearted and had heard a good deal, because he had been talking with Happy Jack. His sympathy was not with the Happy Family, either.

On the second afternoon, such is effect of rigid winnowing, there were but nine men to ride. The fellow who had grabbed the saddle horn, together with ten others, stood among the spectators and made caustic remarks about the management, the horses, the nine who were left and the whole business in general. Andy grinned a little and wondered if he would stand among them on the morrow and make remarks. He was not worrying about it, though. He said hello to Weary, Pink and Cal Emmett, and saddled a kicking, striking brute from up Sweetgrass way.

On this day the horses were wickeder, and one man came near getting his neck broken. As it was, his collar-bone snapped and he was carried off the infield on a stretcher and hurried to the hospital; which did not tend to make the other riders feel more cheerful. Andy noted that it was the HS sorrel which did the mischief, and glanced meaningly across at Billy Roberts.

Then it was his turn with the striking, kicking gray, and he mounted and prepared for what might come. The gray was an artist in his line, and pitched "high, wide and crooked" in the most approved fashion. But Andy, being also an artist of a sort, rode easily and with a grace that brought much hand-clapping from the crowd. Only the initiated reserved their praise till further trial; for though the gray was not to say gentle, and though it took skill to ride him, there were a dozen, probably twice as many, men in the crowd who could have done as well.

The Happy Family, drawn together from habit and because they could speak their minds more freely, discussed Andy gravely among themselves. Betting was growing brisk, and if their faith had not been so shaken they could have got long odds on Andy.

"I betche he don't win out," Happy Jack insisted with characteristic gloom. "Yuh wait till he goes up agin that blue roan. They're savin' that roan till the las' day—and I betche Andy'll git him. If he hangs on till the las' day." Happy Jack laughed ironically as he made the provision.

"Any you fellows got money yuh want to put up on this deal?" came the voice of Andy behind them.

They turned, a bit shamefaced, toward him.

"Aw, I betche—" began Happy.

"That's what I'm here for," cut in Andy. "What I've got goes up—saddle, spurs—*all* I've got. You've done a lot uh mourning, now here's a chance to break even on *me*. Speak up."

The Happy Family hesitated.

"I guess I'll stay out," dimpled Pink. "I don't just savvy your play, Andy, and if I lose on yuh—why, it won't be the first time I ever went broke."

"Well, by golly, *I'll* take a chance," bellowed Slim, whose voice was ever pitched to carry long distances in a high wind. "I'll bet yuh fifty dollars yuh don't pull down that belt or purse. By golly, there's two or three men here that can *ride*."

"There's only one that'll be the real star," smiled Andy with unashamed egotism. "Happy, how rich do *you* want to get off me?"

Happy said a good deal and "betche" several things would happen—things utterly inconsistent with one another. In the end, Andy pinned him down to twenty dollars against Andy's silver-mounted spurs—which was almost a third more than the spurs were worth; but Andy had no sympathy for Happy Jack and stuck to the price doggedly until Happy gave in.

Jack Bates advertised his lack of faith in Andy ten dollars worth, and Cal Emmett did the same. Irish, coming in on the afternoon train and drifting instinctively to the vicinity of the Happy Family, cursed them all impartially for a bunch of quitters, slapped Andy on the back and with characteristic impetuosity offered a hundred dollars to anybody who dared take him up, that Andy would win. And this after he had heard the tale of the blue roan and before they told him about the two rides already made in the contest.

It is true that Happy Jack endeavored to expostulate, but Irish glared at him in a way to make Happy squirm and stammer incoherently.

"I've heard all about it," Irish cut in, "and I don't have to hear any more. I know a rider when I see one, and my money's on Andy from start to finish. You make me sick. Weary, have *you* gone against our man?" The tone was a challenge in itself.

Weary grinned goodnaturedly. "I haven't pulled down any bets," he answered mildly, "and I haven't put up my last cent and don't intend to. I'm an engaged young man." He shrugged his shoulders to point the moral. "I sure do hope Andy'll win out," he added simply.

"*Hope*? Why, damn it, yuh *know* he'll win!" stormed Irish.

Men in their vicinity caught the belligerence of the tone and turned about, thinking there was trouble, and the Happy Family subsided into quieter discussion. In the end Irish, discovering that Andy had for the time being forsworn the shelter of the Flying U tents, stuck by him loyally and forswore it also, and went with Andy to share the doubtful comfort of the obscure lodging house. For Irish was all or nothing, and to find the Happy Family publicly opposed—or at most neutral—to a Flying U man in a rough-riding contest like this, incensed him much.

The Happy Family began to feel less sure of themselves and a bit ashamed— though of just what, they were not quite clear, for surely they had reason a-plenty for doubting Andy Green.

The last day found the Happy Family divided against itself and growing a bit venomous in its remarks. Andy had not as yet done anything remarkable, except perhaps keep in the running when the twenty had been culled to three: Billy Roberts, Andy and a man from the Yellowstone Valley, called Gopher by his acquaintances. Accident and untoward circumstances had thrown out the others—good riders all of them, or they would not have been there. Happy Jack proclaimed loudly in camp that Andy was still in because Andy had not had a real bad horse. "I seen Coleman looking over the blue roan and talkin' to them guys that runs things; they're goin' t' put Andy on him t-day, I betche—and we seen how he can *ride* him! Piled in a heap—"

"Not exactly," Pink interrupted. "I seem to remember Andy lighting on his feet; and he was smoking when he started, and smoking when he quit. It didn't strike me at the time, but that's kinda funny, don't yuh think?"

So Pink went back to his first faith, and the Happy Family straightway became loud and excited over the question of whether Andy did really light upon his feet, or jumped up immediately, and whether he kept his cigarette or made a new one. The discussion carried them to the fair grounds and remained just where it started, so far as any amicable decision was concerned.

Now this is a fair and true report of that last day's riding: There being but the three riders, and the excitement growing apace, the rough-riding was put first on the program and men struggled for the best places and the best view of the infield.

In the beginning, Andy drew the HS sorrel and Billy Roberts the blue roan. Gopher, the Yellowstone man, got a sulky little buckskin that refused to add one whit to the excitement, so that he was put back and another one brought. This other proved to be the wicked-eyed brown which Andy had ridden the first day. Only this day the brown was in different mood and pitched so viciously that Gopher lost control in the rapid-fire changes, and rode wild, being all over the horse and everywhere but on the ground. He did not pull leather, however though he was accused by some of riding on his spurs at the last. At any rate, Andy and Billy Roberts felt that the belt lay between themselves, and admitted as much privately.

"You've sure got to ride like a wild man if yuh beat me to it," grinned Billy.

"By gracious, I'm after it like a wolf myself," Andy retorted. "Yuh know how I'm fixed—I've just got to have it, Bill."

Billy, going out to ride, made no reply except a meaning head-shake. And Billy certainly rode, that day; for the blue roan did his worst and his best. To describe the performance, however, would be to invent many words to supply a dearth in the language. Billy rode the blue roan back to the corral, and he had broken none of the stringent rules of the contest—which is saying much for Billy.

When Andy went out—shot out, one might say—on the sorrel, the Happy Family considered him already beaten because of the remarkable riding of Billy. When the sorrel began pitching the gaping populace, grown wise overnight in these things, said that he was *e-a-s-y*—which he was not. He fought as some men fight; with brain as well as muscle, cunningly, malignantly. He would stop and stand perfectly still for a few seconds, and then spring viciously whichever way would seem to him most unexpected; for he was not bucking from fright as most horses do but because he hated men and would do them injury if he could.

When the crowd thought him worn out, so that he stood with head drooping all that Andy would permit, then it was that Andy grew most wary. It was as he had said. Of a sudden, straight into the air leaped the sorrel, reared and went backward in a flash of red. But as he went, his rider slipped to one side, and when he struck the ground Andy struck also—on his feet. "Get up, darn yuh," he muttered, and when the sorrel gathered himself together and jumped up, he was much surprised to find Andy in the saddle again.

Then it was that the HS sorrel went mad and pitched as he had never, even when building his record, pitched before. Then it was that Andy, his own temper a bit roughened by the murderous brute, rode as he had not ridden for many a day; down in the saddle, his quirt keeping time with the jumps. He was just settling himself to "drag it out of him proper," when one of the judges, on horseback in the field, threw up his hand.

"Get off!" he shouted, galloping closer. "That horse's got to be rode again to-day. You've done enough this time."

So Andy, watching his chance, jumped off when the sorrel stopped for a few seconds of breath, and left him unconquered and more murderous than ever. A man with a megaphone was announcing that the contest was yet undecided, and that Green and Roberts would ride again later in the afternoon.

Andy passed the Happy Family head in air, stopped a minute to exchange facetious threats with Billy Roberts, and went with Irish to roost upon the fence near the judge's stand to watch the races. The Happy Family kept sedulously away from the two and tried to grow interested in other things until the final test.

It came, when Billy Roberts, again first, mounted the HS sorrel, still in murderous mood and but little the worse for his previous battle. What he had done with

Andy he repeated, and added much venom to the repetition. Again he threw himself backward, which Billy expected and so got clear and remounted as he scrambled up. After that, the sorrel simply pitched so hard and so fast that he loosened Billy a bit; not much, but enough to "show daylight" between rider and saddle for two or three high, crooked jumps. One stirrup he lost, rode a jump without it and by good luck regained it as it flew against his foot. It was great riding, and a gratifying roar of applause swept out to him when it was over.

Andy, saddling the blue roan, drew a long breath. This one ride would tell the tale, and he was human enough to feel a nervous strain such as had not before assailed him. It was so close, now! and it might soon be so far. A bit of bad luck such as may come to any man, however great his skill, and the belt would go to Billy. But not for long could doubt or questioning hold Andy Green. He led the Weaver out himself, and instinctively he felt that the horse remembered him and would try all that was in him. Also, he was somehow convinced that the blue roan held much in reserve, and that it would be a great fight between them for mastery.

When he gathered up the reins, the roan eyed him wickedly sidelong and tightened his muscles, as it were, for the struggle. Andy turned the stirrup, put in his toe, and went up in a flash, warned by something in the blue roan's watchful eye. Like a flash the blue roan also went up—but Andy had been a fraction of a second quicker. There was a squeal that carried to the grand stand as the Weaver, wild-eyed and with red flaring nostrils, pounded the wind-baked sod with high, bone-racking jumps; changed and took to "weaving" till one wondered how he kept his footing—more particularly, how Andy contrived to sit there, loose-reined, firm-seated, riding easily. The roan, tiring of that, began "swapping ends" furiously and so fast one could scarce follow his jumps. Andy, with a whoop of pure defiance, yanked off his hat and beat the roan over the head with it, yelling taunting words and contemptuous; and for every shout the Weaver bucked harder and higher, bawling like a new-weaned calf.

Men who knew good riding when they saw it went silly and yelled and yelled. Those who did not know anything about it caught the infection and roared. The judges galloped about, backing away from the living whirlwind and yelling with the rest. Came a lull when the roan stood still because he lacked breath to continue, and the judges shouted an uneven chorus.

"Get down—the belt's yours"—or words to that effect. It was unofficial, that verdict, but it was unanimous and voiced with enthusiasm.

Andy turned his head and smiled acknowledgment. "All right—but wait till I tame this hoss proper! Him and I've got a point to settle!" He dug in his spurs and again the battle raged, and again the crowd, not having heard the unofficial decision, howled and yelled approval of the spectacle.

Not till the roan gave up completely and owned obedience to rein and voiced command, did Andy take further thought of the reward. He satisfied himself beyond doubt that he was master and that the Weaver recognized him as such. He wheeled and turned, "cutting out" an imaginary animal from an imaginary herd; he loped and he walked, stopped dead still in two jumps and started in one. He leaned and ran his gloved hand forgivingly along the slatey blue neck, reached farther and pulled facetiously the roan's ears, and the roan meekly permitted the liberties. He half turned in the saddle and slapped the plump hips, and the Weaver never moved. "Why, you're an all-right little hoss!" praised Andy, slapping again and again.

The decision was being bellowed from the megaphone and Andy, hearing it thus officially, trotted over to where a man was holding out the belt that proclaimed him champion of the state. Andy reached out a hand for the belt, buckled it around his middle and saluted the grand stand as he used to do from the circus ring when one André de Grenó had performed his most difficult feat.

The Happy Family crowded up, shamefaced and manfully willing to own themselves wrong.

"We're down and ready to be walked on by the Champion," Weary announced quizzically. "Mama mine! but yuh sure can ride."

Andy looked at them, grinned and did an exceedingly foolish thing, just to humiliate Happy Jack, who, he afterwards said, still looked unconvinced. He coolly got upon his feet in the saddle, stood so while he saluted the Happy Family mockingly, lighted the cigarette he had just rolled, then, with another derisive salute, turned a double somersault in the air and lighted upon his feet—and the roan did nothing more belligerent than to turn his head and eye Andy suspiciously.

"By gracious, maybe you fellows'll some day own up yuh don't know it all!" he cried, and led the Weaver back into the corral and away from the whooping maniacs across the track.

ANDY, THE LIAR

Andy Green licked a cigarette into shape the while he watched with unfriendly eyes the shambling departure of their guest. "I believe the darned old reprobate was lyin' to us," he remarked, when the horseman disappeared into a coulee.

"You sure ought to be qualified to recognize the symptoms," grunted Cal Emmett, kicking his foot out of somebody's carelessly coiled rope on the ground. "That your rope, Happy? No wonder you're always on the bum for one. If you'd try tying it on your saddle—"

"Aw, g'wan. That there's Andy's rope—"

"If you look at my saddle, you'll find my rope right where it belongs," Andy retorted. "I ain't sheepherder enough to leave it kicking around under foot. That rope belongs to his nibs that just rode off. When he caught up his horse again after dinner, he throwed his rope down while he saddled up, and then went off and forgot it. He wasn't easy in his mind—that jasper wasn't. I don't go very high on that hard-luck tale he told. I know the boy he had wolfing with him last winter, and he wasn't the kind to pull out with all the stuff he could get his hands on. He was an all-right fellow, and if there's been any rusty work done down there in the breaks, this shifty-eyed mark done it. He was lying—"

Somebody laughed suddenly, and another chuckle helped to point the joke, until the whole outfit was in an uproar; for of all the men who had slept under Flying-U tents and eaten beside the mess-wagon, Andy Green was conceded to be the greatest, the most shameless and wholly incorrigible liar of the lot.

"Aw, yuh don't want to get jealous of an old stiff like that," Pink soothed musically. "There ain't one of us but what knows you could lie faster and farther and more of it in a minute, with your tongue half-hitched around your palate and the deaf-and-dumb language barred, than any three men in Chouteau County. Don't let it worry yuh, Andy."

"I ain't letting it worry me," said Andy, getting a bit red with trying not to show that the shot hit him. "When my imagination gets to soaring, I'm willing to bet all I got that it can fly higher than the rest of you, that have got brains about on a par with a sage-hen, can follow. When I let my fancy soar, I take notice the rest of yuh like to set in the front row, all right—and yuh never, to my knowledge, called it a punk show when the curtain rung down; yuh always got the worth uh your money, and then some.

"But if yuh'd taken notice of the load that old freak was trying to throw into the bunch, you'd suspicion there was something scaley about it; there was, all right. I'd gamble on it."

"From the symptoms," spoke Weary mildly, rising to an elbow, "Andy's about to erupt one of those wide, hot, rushing streams of melted imagination that bursts forth from his think-works ever so often. Don't get us all worked up over it, Andy; what's it going to be this time? A murder in the Bad-lands?"

Andy clicked his teeth together, thought better of his ill-humor and made re-ply, though he had intended to remain dignifiedly silent.

"Yuh rung the bell, m'son—but it ain't any josh. By gracious, I mean it!" He glared at those who gurgled incredulously, and went on: "No, sir, you bet it ain't any josh with me *this* time. That old gazabo had something heavy on his conscience—and knowing the fellow he had reference to, I sure believe he lied a whole lot when he said Dan pulled out with all the stuff they'd got together, and went down river. Maybe he went down river, all right—but if he did, it was most likely to be face-down. Dan was as honest a boy as there is in the country, and he had money on him that he got mining down in the little Rockies last summer. I know, because he showed me the stuff last fall when I met him in Benton, and he was fixing to winter with this fellow that just left.

"Dan was kinda queer about some things, and one of 'em was about money. It never made any difference how much or how little he had, he always packed it in his clothes; said a bank had busted on him once and left him broke in the middle uh winter, and he wasn't going to let it happen again. He never gambled none, nor blowed his money any farther than a couple uh glasses uh beer once in a while. He was one uh these saving cusses—but he was honest; I know that for a fact.

"So he had all this money on him, and went down there with this jasper, that he'd got in with somehow and didn't know much about, and they wolfed all win-ter, according to all accounts, and must uh made quite a stake, the way the bounty runs up, these days. And here comes this darned Siwash, hiking out uh there fast as he can—and if he hadn't run slap onto us at this crossing, I'll gamble he'd never uh showed up at camp at all, but kept right on going. We didn't ask him no ques-tions, did we? But he goes to all the pains uh telling us his tale uh woe, about how Dan had robbed him and pulled out down river.

"If that was the case, wouldn't he be apt to hike out after him and try and get back his stuff? And wouldn't—"

"How much money did this friend uh yours have?" queried Jack Bates inno-cently.

"Well, when I seen him in Benton, he had somewhere between six and seven hundred dollars. He got it all changed into fifty-dollar bills—"

"Oh, golly!" Jack Bates rolled over in disgust. "Andy's losing his grip. Why, darn yuh, if you was in a normal, lying condition, you'd make it ten thousand, at the lowest—and I've seen the time when you'd uh said fifty thousand; and you'd uh made us swallow the load, too! Buck up and do a good stunt, Andy, or else keep still. Why, Happy Jack could tell that big a lie!"

"Aw, gwan!" Happy Jack rose up to avenge the insult. "Yuh needn't compare me to Andy Green. I ain't a liar, and I can lick the darned son-of-a-gun that calls me one. I ain't, and yuh can't say I am, unless yuh lie worse'n Andy."

"Calm down," urged Weary pacifically. "Jack said yuh *could* lie; he didn't say—"

"By gracious, you'd think I was necked up with a whole bunch uh George Washingtons!" growled Andy, half-indignantly. "And what gets me is, that I tell the truth as often as anybody in the outfit; oftener than some I could mention. But that ain't the point. I'm telling the truth now, when I say somebody ought to hike down to their camp and see what this old skunk has done with Dan. I'd bet money you'd find him sunk in the river, or cached under a cut-bank, or something like that. If he'd kept his face closed I wouldn't uh give it a second thought, but the more I think uh the story he put up, the more I believe there's something wrong. He's made way with Dan somehow, and—"

"Yes. Sure thing," drawled Pink wickedly. "Let's organize a searching party and go down there and investigate. It's only about a three or four days' trip, through the roughest country the Lord ever stood on end to cool and then forgot till it crumpled down in spots and got set that way, so He just left it go and mixed fresh mud for the job He was working on. Andy'd lead us down there, and we'd find—"

"His friend Dan buried in a tomato can, maybe," supplied Jack Bates.

"By golly, I'll bet yuh *could* put friend Dan into one," Slim burst out. "By golly, *I* never met up with no Dan that packed fifty-dollar bills around in his gun-pocket—"

"Andy's telling the truth. He says so," reproved Weary. "And when Andy says a thing is the truth, yuh always know—"

"It ain't." Cal Emmett finished the sentence, but Weary paid no attention.

"—what to expect. Cadwolloper's right, and we ought to go down there and make a hunt for friend Dan and his fifty-dollar bills. How many were there, did yuh say?"

"You go to the devil," snapped Andy, getting up determinedly. "Yuh bite quick enough when anybody throws a load at yuh that would choke a rhinoscerous, but plain truth seems to be too much for the weak heads of yuh. I guess I'll have to turn loose and *lie*, so yuh'll listen to me. There *is* something crooked about this deal—"

"We all thought it sounded that way," Weary remarked mildly.

"And if yuh did go down to where them two wintered, you'd find out I'm right. But yuh won't, and that old cutthroat will get off with the murder—and the money."

"Don't he lie natural?" queried Jack Bates solemnly.

That was too much. Andy glared angrily at the group, picked up the wolfer's rope, turned on his heel and walked off to where his horse was tied; got on him and rode away without once looking back, though he knew quite well that they were watching every move he made. It did not help to smooth his temper that the sound of much laughing followed him as he swung into the trail taken by the man who had left not long before.

Where he went, that afternoon when for some reason sufficient for the fore-man—who was Chip Bennett—the Flying U roundup crew lay luxuriously snor-ing in the shade instead of riding hurriedly and hotly the high divides, no one but Andy himself knew. They talked about him after he left, and told one another how great a liar he was, and how he couldn't help it because he was born that way, and how you could hardly help believing him. They recalled joyously certain of his fabrications that had passed into the history of the Flying U, and wondered what josh he was trying to spring this time.

"What we ought to do," advised Cal, "is to lead him on and let him lie his darndest, and make out we believe him. And then we can give him the laugh good and plenty—and maybe cure him."

"Cure nothing!" exclaimed Jack Bates, getting up because the sun had dis-covered him, and going over to the mess-wagon where a bit of shade had been left unoccupied. "About the only way to cure Andy of lying, is to kill him. He was working his way up to some big josh, and if yuh let him alone you'll find out what it is, all right. I wouldn't worry none about it, if I was you." To prove that he did not worry, Jack immediately went to sleep.

Such being the attitude of the Happy Family, when Andy rode hurriedly into camp at sundown, his horse wet to the tips of his ears with sweat, they sat up, ex-pectancy writ large upon their faces. No one said anything, however, while Andy unsaddled and came over to beg a belated supper from the cook; nor yet while he squatted on his heels beside the cook-tent and ate hungrily. He seemed somewhat absorbed in his thoughts, and they decided mentally that Andy was a sure-enough good actor, and that if they were not dead next to him and his particular weakness, they would swallow his yarn whole—whatever it was. A blood-red glow was in the sky to the west, and it lighted Andy's face queerly, like a vivid blush on the face of a girl.

Andy scraped his plate thoughtfully with his knife, looked into his coffee-cup, stirred the dregs absently and dipped out half a spoonful of undissolved sugar, which he swallowed meditatively. He tossed plate, cup and spoon toward the dishpan, sent knife and fork after them and got out his smoking material. And the Happy Family, grouped rather closely together and watching unobtrusively, stirred to the listening point. The liar was about to lie.

"Talk about a guilty conscience giving a man dead away," Andy began, quite unconscious of the mental attitude of his fellows, and forgetting also his anger of the afternoon, "it sure does work out like that, sometimes. I followed that old dev-il, just out uh curiosity, to see if he headed for Dry Lake like he said he was going. *We* didn't have any reason for keeping cases on him, or suspicioning anything— but he acted like we was all out on his trail, the fool!

"I kinda had a hunch that if he had been up to any deviltry, it would show on him when he left here, and I was plumb right about it. He went all straight enough till he got down into Black Coulee; and right there it looked like he got kinda panicky and suspicious, for he turned square off the trail and headed up the coulee."

"He must uh had 'em," Weary commented, quite as if he believed.

"Yuh wait till I'm through," Andy advised, still wholly unconscious of their disbelief. "Yuh was all kinda skeptical when I told yuh he had a guilty conscience, but I was right about it, and come mighty near laying out on the range to-night with my toes pointing straight up, just because you fellows wouldn't—"

"Sun-stroke?" asked Pink, coming closer, his eyes showing purple in the softened light.

"No—yuh wait, now, till I tell yuh." Whereupon Andy smoked relishfully and in silence, and from the tail of his eye watched his audience squirm with impatience. "A man gets along a whole lot better without any conscience," he began at last, irrelevantly, "'specially if he wants to be mean. I trailed this jasper up the coulee and out on the bench, across that level strip between Black Coulee and Dry Spring Gulch, and down the gulch a mile or so. He was fogging right along, and seemed as if he looked back every ten rods—I know he spotted me just as I struck the level at the head uh Black Coulee, because he acted different then.

"I could see he was making across country for the trail to Chinook, but I wanted to overhaul him and have a little casual talk about Dan. I don't suppose yuh noticed I took his rope along; I wanted some excuse for hazing after him like that, yuh see."

"Uh course, such accommodating cusses as you wouldn't be none strange to him," fleered Cal.

"Well, he never found out what I was after," sighed Andy. "It wasn't my fault I didn't come up with him, and my intentions were peaceful and innocent. But do yuh know what happened? He got out uh sight down Dry Spring Gulch—yuh know where that elephant-head rock sticks out, and the trail makes a short turn around it—that's where I lost sight of him. But he wasn't very far in the lead, and I was dead anxious to give him his rope, so I loped on down—"

"You were taking long chances, old-timer; that's mighty rough going, along there," hinted Chip, gravely.

"Sure, I was," Andy agreed easily. "But yuh recollect, I was in a hurry. So I'd just rounded the elephant's head, when *bing!* something spats the rock, just over my right shoulder, and my horse squatted down on his rump and said he'd gone far enough. I kinda felt the same way about it, so when he wheeled and humped himself back up the trail, I didn't argue none with him."

There was silence so deep one could hear the saddle-bunch cropping the thick grasses along the creek. If this were true—this tale that Andy was telling—The Happy Family, half tempted to believe, glanced furtively at one another.

"Aw, gwan!" It was the familiar, protesting croak of Happy Jack. "What did yuh turn tail for? Why didn't yuh have it out with him?" The Happy Family drew a long breath, and the temptation to believe was pushed aside.

"Because my gun was rolled up in my bed," Andy replied simply. "I ain't as brave as you are, Happy. I ain't got the nerve to ride right up on a man that's scared plumb silly and pumping lead my way fast as he can work the lever on his rifle, and lick him with my fists till he howls, and then throw him and walk up and down his person and flap my wings and crow. It's awful to have to confess it, but I'm willing to run from any man that's shooting at me when I can't shoot back. I'd give a lot to be as brave as you are, Happy."

Happy Jack growled and subsided.

"Well, by golly, there's times when *we'd* be justified in shooting yuh, but I don't see what *he'd* want to do it for," objected Slim.

"Guilty conscience, I told yuh," retorted Andy. "He seen I was chasing him up, and I guess he thought it was somebody that had got next to what happened— Lord, I wish I knew what did happen, down there in the breaks! Boys," Andy got up and stood looking earnestly down at them in the twilight, "you can't make me believe that there hasn't been a murder done! That fellow has been up to something, or he wouldn't be acting so damn' queer. And if it was just plain stealing, Dan would sure be hot on his trail—because Dan thought more of his money than most men do of their wives. It was about all he lived for, and he wasn't any coward. That old man never would get it off him without a big ruction, and if he did, Dan would be right after him bigger'n a wolf. There's something wrong, you take my word."

"What do yuh want us to do about it?" It was Chip who asked the question, and his tone was quite calm and impersonal.

Andy looked at him reproachfully. "Do? What is there to do, except go down there and see? If we can find that out, we can put the sheriff wise and let him do the rest. It sure does seem kinda tough, if a man can do a murder and robbery and get off with it, just because nobody cares enough about it to head him off."

The Happy Family stirred uneasily. Of course, it was all just a josh of Andy's— but he was such a convincing liar! Almost they felt guilty of criminal negligence that they did not at once saddle up and give chase to the murderer, who had tried to kill Andy for following him, and who was headed for Chinook after unnecessarily proclaiming himself bound for Dry Lake.

"Do you want the whole outfit to turn out?" asked Chip calmly at last.

"No-o—"

"Say, is it anywheres near that prehistoric castle you found once?" Ping asked maliciously, unbelief getting strong hold of him again.

Andy turned toward him, scowling. "No, Angel-child, it ain't," he snapped. "And you fellows can back up and snort all yuh darn please, and make idiots of yourselves. But yuh can't do any business making me out a hot-air peddler on *this* deal. I stand pat, just where I stood at first, and it'll take a lot uh cackling to make me back down. That old devil *did* lie about Dan, and he did take a shot at me—"

"He took yuh for a horse-thief, most likely," explained Jack Bates.

"He didn't need no field glass to see you was a suspicious character, by golly," chortled Slim.

"He thought yuh was after what little your friend Dan had overlooked, chances is," added Cal Emmett.

"Did the fog roll down and hide the horrible sight?" asked Jack Bates.

That, and much more, brought about a distinct coldness between the Happy Family and one Andy Green, so that the sun went down upon Andy's wrath, and rose to find it still bubbling hotly in the outraged heart of him.

It was Jack Bates who precipitated an open war by singing an adapted version of "Massa's In the Cold, Cold Ground," just when they were eating breakfast. As an alleged musical effort it was bad enough, but as a personal insult it was worse. One hesitates to repeat the doggerel, even in an effort to be exact. However, the chorus, bellowed shamelessly by Jack, was this:

"Down in the Bad-lands, hear that awful sound.
Andy Green is there a-weeping—"

Jack Bates got no further than that, for Andy first threw his plate at Jack and then landed upon him with much force and venom, so that Jack went backwards and waved long legs convulsively in the air, and the Happy Family stood around and howled their appreciation of the spectacle.

When it dawned upon them that Andy was very much in earnest, and that his fist was landing with unpleasant frequency just where it was most painful to receive it, they separated the two by main strength and argued loudly for peace. But Andy was thoroughly roused and would have none of it, and hurled at them profanity and insulting epithets, so that more than Jack Bates looked upon him with unfriendly eyes and said things which were not calculated to smooth roughened tempers.

"That's a-plenty, now," quelled Chip, laying detaining hand upon the nearest, who happened to be Andy himself. "You sound like a bunch of old women. What do you want to do the worst and quickest, Andy?—and I don't mean killing off any of these alleged joshers, either."

Andy clicked his teeth together, swallowed hard and slowly unclenched his hands and grinned; but the grin was not altogether a pleasant one, and the light of battle still shone in the big, gray eyes of him.

"You're the boss," he said, "but if yuh don't like my plans you'll just have one less to pay wages to. What I'm going to do is throw my saddle on my private horse and ride down into the Bad-lands and see for myself how the cards lay. Maybe it's awful funny to the rest of yuh, but I'm takin' it kinda serious, myself, and I'm going to find out how about it before I'm through. I can't seem to think it's a josh when some old mark makes a play like that fellow did, and tries to put a bullet into my carcass for riding the same trail he took. It's me for the Bad-lands—and you can think what yuh damn' please about it."

Chip stood quite still till he was through, and eyed him sharply. "You better take old Buck to pack your blankets and grub," he told him, in a matter-of-fact tone. "We'll be swinging down that way in two or three days; by next Saturday you'll find us camped at the mouth of Jump-off Coulee, if nothing happens. That'll give you four days to prowl around. Come on, boys—we've got a big circle ahead of us this morning, and it's going to be hot enough to singe the tails off our cayuses by noon."

That, of course, settled the disturbance and set the official seal of approval upon Andy's going; for Chip was too wise to permit the affair to grow serious, and perhaps lose a man as good as Andy; family quarrels had not been entirely unknown among the boys of the Flying U, and with tact they never had been more than a passing unpleasantness. So that, although Jack Bates swore vengeance and nursed sundry bruised spots on his face, and though Andy saddled, packed old Buck with his blankets and meager camp outfit and rode off sullenly with no word to anyone and only a scowling glance or two for farewell, Chip mounted and rode cheerfully away at the head of his Happy Family, worrying not at all over the outcome.

"I've got half a notion that Andy was telling the truth, after all," he remarked to Weary when they were well away from camp. "It's worth taking a chance on, anyhow—and when he comes back things will be smooth again."

When Saturday came and brought no Andy to camp, the Happy Family began to speculate upon his absence. When Sunday's circle took them within twelve or fifteen miles of the camp in the Bad-lands, Pink suddenly proposed that they ride down there and see what was going on. "He won't be looking for us," he explained, to hide a secret uneasiness. "And if he's there we can find out what the josh is. If he ain't, we'll have it on him good and strong."

"I betche Andy just wanted a lay-off, and took that way uh getting it," declared Happy Jack pessimistically. "I betche he's in town right now, tearing things wide open and tickled to think he don't have to ride in this hot sun. Yuh can't never tell what Andy's got cached up his sleeve."

"Chip thinks he was talking on the level," Weary mused. "Maybe he was; as Happy says, yuh can't tell."

As always before, this brought the Happy Family to argument which lasted till they neared the deep, lonely coulee where, according to Andy, "friend Dan" had wintered with the shifty-eyed old man.

"Now, how the mischief do we get down?" questioned Jack Bates complainingly. "This is bound to be the right place—there's the cabin over there against the cottonwoods."

"Aw, come on back," urged Happy Jack, viewing the steep bluff with disfavor. "Chances is, Andy's in town right now. He ain't down—"

"There's old Buck, over there by the creek," Pink announced. "I'd know him far as I could see him. Let's ride around that way. There's sure to be a trail down." He started off, and they followed him dispiritedly, for the heat was something to remember afterwards with a shudder.

"Here's the place," Pink called back to them, after some minutes of riding. "Andy's horse is down there, too, but I don't see Andy—"

"Chances is—" began Happy Jack, but found no one listening.

It would be impossible to ride down, so they dismounted and prepared for the scramble. They could see Buck, packed as if for the homeward trail, and they could see Andy's horse, saddled and feeding with reins dragging. He looked up at them and whinnied, and the sound but accentuated the loneliness of the place. Buck, too, saw them and came toward them, whinnying wistfully; but, though they strained eyes in every direction, they could see nothing of the man they sought.

It was significant of their apprehension that not even Happy Jack made open comment upon the strangeness of it. Instead, they dug bootheels deep where the slope was loose gravel, and watched that their horses did not slide down upon them; climbed over rocks where the way was barred, and prayed that horse and man might not break a leg. They had been over rough spots, and had climbed in and out of deep coulees, but never had they travelled a rougher trail than that.

"My God! boys, look down there!" Pink cried, when yet fifty perpendicular feet lay between them and the level below.

They looked, and drew breath sharply. Huddled at the very foot of the last and worst slope lay Andy, and they needed no words to explain what had happened. It was evident that he had started to climb the bluff and had slipped and fallen to the bottom, And from the way he was lying—The Happy Family shut out the horror of the thought and hurried recklessly to the place.

It was Pink who, with a last slide and a stumbling recovery at the bottom, reached him first. It was Jack Bates who came a close second and helped to turn him—for he had fallen partly on his face. From the way one arm was crumpled back under him, they knew it to be broken. Further than that they could only guess and hope. While they were feeling for heart-beats, the others came down and crowded close. Pink looked up at them strainedly.

"Oh, for God's sake, some of yuh get water," he cried sharply. "What good do yuh think you're doing, just standing around?"

"We ought to be hung for letting him come down here alone," Weary repented. "It ain't safe for one man in this cursed country. Where's he hurt, Cadwolloper?"

"How in hell do *I* know?" Anxiety ever sharpened the tongue of Pink. "If somebody'd bring some water—"

"Happy's gone. And there ain't a drop uh whisky in the crowd! Can't we get him into the shade? This damned sun is enough to—"

"Look out how yuh lift him, man! You ain't wrassling a calf, remember! You take his shoulder, Jack—*easy*, yuh damned, awkward—"

"Here comes Happy, with his hat full. Don't slosh it all on at once! A little at a time's better. Get some on his head."

So with much incoherence and with everybody giving orders and each acting independently, they bore him tenderly into the shade of a rock and worked over him feverishly, their faces paler than his. When he opened his eyes and stared at them dully, they could have shouted for very relief. When he closed them again they bent over him solicitously and dripped more water from the hat of Happy Jack. And not one of them but remembered remorsefully the things they had said of him, not an hour before; the things they had said even when he was lying there alone and hurt—hurt unto death, for all they knew.

When he was roused enough to groan when they moved him, however gently, they began to consider the problem of getting him to camp, and they cursed the long, hot miles that lay between. They tried to question him, but if he understood what they were saying he could not reply except by moaning, which was not good to hear. All that they could gather was that when they moved his body in a certain way the pain of it was unbearable. Also, he would faint when his head was lowered, or even lifted above the level. They must guard against that if they meant to get him to camp alive.

"We'll have to carry him up this cussed hill, and then—If he could ride at all, we might make it."

"The chances is he'll die on the road," croaked Happy Jack tactlessly, and they scowled at him for voicing the fear they were trying to ignore. They had been trying not to think that he might die on the road, and they had been careful not to mention the possibility. As it was, no one answered.

How they ever got him to the top of that heartbreaking slope, not one of them ever knew. Twice he fainted outright. And Happy Jack, carefully bearing his hat full of water for just that emergency, slipped and spilled the whole of it just when they needed it most. At the last, it was as if they carried a dead man between them—Jack Bates and Cal Emmett it was who bore him up the last steep climb—and Pink and Weary, coming behind with all the horses, glanced fearfully into each other's eyes and dared not question.

At the top they laid him down in the grass and swore at Happy Jack, because they must do something, and because they dared not face what might be before them. They avoided looking at one another while they stood helplessly beside the still figure of the man they had maligned. If he died, they would always have that bitter spot in their memory—and even with the fear of his dying they stood remorseful.

Of a sudden Andy opened his eyes and looked at them with the light of recognition, and they bent eagerly toward him. "If—yuh could—on—my horse—I—I—could ride—maybe." Much pain it cost him, they knew by the look on his face. But he was game to the last—just as they knew he would be.

"Yuh couldn't ride Twister, yuh know yuh couldn't," Pink objected gently. "But—if yuh could ride Jack's horse—he's dead gentle, and we'd help hold yuh on. Do you think yuh could?"

Andy moved his head uneasily. "I—I've got to," he retorted weakly, and even essayed a smile to reassure them. "I—ain't all—in yet," he added with an evident effort, and the Happy Family gulped sympathetically, and wondered secretly if they would have such nerve under like conditions.

"It's going to be one hell of a trip for yuh," Weary murmured commiseratingly, when they were lifting him into the saddle. Of a truth, it did seem absolutely foolhardy to attempt it, but there was nothing else to do, unless they left him there. For no wagon could possibly be driven within miles of the place.

Andy leaned limply over the saddle-horn, his face working with the agony he suffered. Somehow they had got him upon the horse of Jack Bates, but they had felt like torturers while they did it, and the perspiration on their faces was not all caused by heat.

"My God, I'd rather be hung than go through this again," muttered Cal, white under the tan. "I—"

"I'll tackle—it now," gasped Andy, with a pitiful attempt to sit straight in the saddle. "Get on—boys—"

Reluctantly they started to obey, when the horse of Jack Bates gave a sudden leap ahead. Many hands reached out to grasp him by the bridle, but they were a shade too late, and he started to run, with Andy swaying in the saddle. While they gazed horrified, he straightened convulsively, turned his face toward them and raised a hand; caught his hat by the brim and swung it high above his head.

"Much obliged, boys," he yelled derisively. "I sure do appreciate being packed up that hill; it was too blamed hot to walk. Say! if you'd gone around that bend, you'd uh found a good trail down. Yuh struck about the worst place there is. So-long—I ain't all in yet!" He galloped away, while the Happy Family stared after him with bulging eyes.

"The son-of-a-gun!" gasped Weary weakly, and started for his horse.

"Darn yuh, you'll *be* all in when we get hold of yuh!" screamed Jack Bates, and gave chase.

It was when they were tearing headlong after him down the coulee's rim and into a shallow gully which seamed unexpectedly the level, that they saw his horse swerve suddenly and go bounding along the edge of the slope with Andy "sawing" energetically upon the bit.

"What trick's he up to now?" cried Cal Emmett resentfully, feeling that, in the light of what had gone before, Andy could not possibly make a single motion in good faith.

Andy brought his horse under control and turned back to meet them, and the Happy Family watched him guardedly until they reached the gulley and their own horses took fright at a dark, shambling object that scuttled away down toward the coulee-head. Andy was almost upon them before they could give him any attention.

"Did you see it?" he called excitedly. "It was a bear, and he was digging at something under that shelving rock. Come on and let's take a look."

"Aw, gwan!" Happy Jack adjured crossly. He was thinking of all the water he had carried painstakingly in his hat, for the relief of this conscienceless young reprobate, and he was patently suspicious of some new trick.

"Well, by gracious!" Andy rode quite close—dangerously close, considering the mood they were in—and eyed them queerly. "I sure must have a horrible rep, when yuh won't believe your own eyes just because I happen to remark that a bear is a bear. I'll call it a pinto hog, if it'll make yuh feel any better. And I'll say it wasn't doing any digging; only, I'm going down there and take a look. There's an odor—"

There was, and they could not deny it, even though Andy did make the assertion. And though they had threatened much that was exceedingly unpleasant, and what they would surely do to Andy if they ever got him within reach, they followed him quite peaceably.

They saw him get off his horse and stand looking down at something—and there was that in his attitude which made them jab spurs against their horses' flanks. A moment later they, too, were looking down at something, and they were not saying a word.

"It's Dan, all right," said Andy at last, and his tone was hushed. "I hunted the coulee over—every foot of it—and looked up some of the little draws, and went along the river; but I couldn't find any trace of him. I never thought about coming up here.

"Look there. His head was smashed in with a rock or something—ugh! Here, let me away, boys.

This thing—" He walked uncertainly away and sat down upon a rock with his face in his hands, and what they could see of his face was as white as the tan would permit. Somehow, not a man of them doubted him then. And not a man of them but felt much the same. They backed away and stood close to where Andy was sitting.

"You wouldn't believe me when I told yuh," he reproached, when the sickness had passed and he could lift his head and look at them. "You thought I was lying, and yuh made yourselves pretty blamed obnoxious to me—but I got even for *that*." There was much satisfaction in his tone, and the Happy Family squirmed. "Yuh see, I was telling the truth, all right—and now I'm going to get even some more. I'm going to take—er—Pink along for a witness, and notify the outfit that yuh won't be back for a day or two, and send word to the sheriff. And you jaspers can have the pleasure uh standing guard over—*that*." He shivered a little and turned his glance quickly away. "And I hope," he added maliciously, as he mounted his own horse, "you'll make Jack Bates stand an all-night guard by his high lonesome. He's sure got it coming to him!"

With Pink following close at his heels he rode away up the ridge.

"Say, there's grub enough on old Buck to do yuh to-night," he called down to them, "in case Chip don't send yuh any till to-morrow." He waved a subdued farewell and turned his face again up the ridge, and before they had quite decided what to do about it, he was gone.

"WOLF! WOLF!"

Andy Green, of the Flying U, loped over the grassy level and hummed a tune as he rode. The sun shone just warm enough to make a man feel that the world was good enough for him, and the wind was just a lazy, whispering element to keep the air from growing absolutely still and stagnant. There was blue sky with white, fluffy bits of cloud like torn cotton drifting as lazily as the wind, and there were meadow-larks singing and swaying, and slow-moving range cattle with their calves midway to weaning time. Not often may one ride leisurely afar on so perfect a day, and while Andy was a sunny-natured fellow at all times, on such a day he owned not a care.

A mile farther, and he rode over a low shoulder of the butte he was passing, ambled down the long slope on the far side, crossed another rounded hill, followed down a dry creek-bed at the foot of it, sought with his eye for a practicable crossing and went headlong down a steep, twenty-foot bank; rattled the loose rocks in the dry, narrow channel and went forging up a bank steeper than the first, with creaking saddle-leather and grunting horse, and struck again easy going.

"She slipped on me," he murmured easily, meaning the saddle. "I'm riding on your tail, just about; but I guess we can stand it the rest uh the why, all right." If he had not been so lazy and self-satisfied he would have stopped right there and reset the saddle. But if he had, he might have missed something which he liked to live over o' nights.

He went up a gentle rise, riding slowly because of the saddle, passed over the ridge and went down another short slope. At the foot of the slope, cuddled against another hill, stood a low, sod-roofed cabin with rusty stove-pipe rising aslant from one corner. This was the spot he had been aiming for, and he neared it slowly.

It was like a dozen other log cabins tucked away here and there among the foothills of the Bear Paws. It had an air of rakish hominess, as if it would be a fine, snuggy place in winter, when the snow and the wind swept the barren land around. In the summer, it stood open-doored and open-windowed, with all the litter of bachelor belongings scattered about or hanging from pegs on the wall outside. There was a faint trail of smoke from the rusty pipe, and it brought a grunt of satisfaction from Andy.

"He's home, all right. And if he don't throw together some uh them sourdough biscuits uh his, there'll be something happen! Hope the bean-pot's full. G'wan, yuh lazy old skate." He slapped the rein-ends lightly down the flanks of his horse and went at a trot around the end of the cabin. And there he was so utterly taken by surprise that he almost pulled his mount into a sitting posture.

A young woman was stooping before the open door, and she was pouring something from a white earthen bowl into a battered tin pan. Two waggle-tailed lambs—a black one and a white—were standing on their knees in their absorption, and were noisily drinking of the stuff as fast as it came within reach.

Andy had half a minute in which to gaze before the young woman looked up, said "Oh!" in a breathless sort of way and retreated to the doorstep, where she stood regarding him inquiringly.

Andy, feeling his face go unreasonably red, lifted his hat. He knew that she was waiting for him to speak, but he could not well say any of the things he thought, and blurted out an utterly idiotic question.

"What are yuh feeding 'em?"

The girl looked down at the bowl in her hands and laughed a little.

"Rolled oats," she answered, "boiled very thin and with condensed cream added to taste. Good morning." She seemed about to disappear, and that brought Andy to his senses. He was not, as a rule, a bashful young man.

"Good morning. Is—er—Mr. Johnson at home?" He came near saying "Take-Notice," but caught himself in time. Take-Notice Johnson was what men called the man whom Andy had ridden over to see upon a more or less trivial matter.

"He isn't, but he will be back—if you care to wait." She spoke with a certain preciseness which might be natural or artificial, and she stood in the doorway with no symptoms of immediate disappearance.

Andy slid over a bit in the saddle, readjusted his hat so that its brim would shield his eyes from the sunlight, and prepared to be friendly. "Oh, I'll wait," he said easily. "I've got all the time there is. Would you mind if I smoked a cigarette?"

"Indeed, I was wishing you would," she told him, with surprising frankness. "I've so longed to see a dashing young cowboy roll a cigarette with deft, white fingers."

Andy, glancing at her startled, spilled much tobacco down the front of him, stopped to brush it away and let the lazy breeze snatch the tiny oblong of paper from between his unwatchful fingers. Of course, she was joshing him, he thought uneasily, as he separated the leaves of his cigarette book by blowing gently upon them, and singled out another paper. "Are yuh so new to the country that it's anything of a treat?" he asked guardedly.

"Yes, I'm new. I'm what you people call a pilgrim. Don't you do it with one hand? I thought—oh, yes! You hold the reins between your firm, white teeth while you roll—"

"Lady, I never travelled with no show," Andy protested mildly and untruthfully. *Was* she just joshing? Or didn't she know any better? She looked sober as anything, but somehow her eyes kind of—

"You see, I know some things about you. Those are chaps" (Heavens! She called them the way they are spelled, without the soft sound of s!) "That you're wearing for—trousers" (Andy blushed modestly. He was not wearing them "for trousers".), "and you've got jingling rowels at your heels, and those are taps—"

"You're going to be shy a yard or two of calico if that black lamb-critter has his say-so," Andy cut in remorselessly, and hastily made and lighted his cigarette while she was rescuing her blue calico skirt from the jaws of the black lamb and puckering her eyebrows over the chewed place. When her attention was once more given to him, he was smoking as unobtrusively as possible, and he was gazing at her with a good deal of speculative admiration. He looked hastily down at the lambs. "Mary had *two* little lambs," he murmured inanely.

"They're not mine," she informed him, taking him seriously—or seeming to do so. Andy had some trouble deciding just how much of her was sincere. "They were here when I came, and I can't take them back with me, so there's no use in claiming them. They'd be such a nuisance on the train—"

"I reckon they would," Andy agreed, "if yuh had far to go."

"Well, you can't call San Jose *close*," she observed, meditatively. "It takes four days to come."

"You're a long way from home. Does it—are yuh homesick, ever?" Andy was playing for information without asking directly how long she intended to stay—a question which had suddenly seemed quite important. Also, why was she stopping here with Take-Notice Johnson, away off from everybody?

"Seeing I've only been here four days, the novelty hasn't worn off yet," she replied. "But it does seem more like four weeks; and how I'll ever stand two months of it, not ever seeing a soul but father—"

Andy looked reproachful, and also glad. Didn't she consider him a soul? And Take-Notice was her dad! To be sure, Take-Notice had never mentioned having a daughter, but then, in the range-land, men don't go around yawping their personal affairs.

Before Take-Notice returned, Andy felt that he had accomplished much. He had learned that the young woman's name really was Mary, and that she was a stenographer in a real-estate office in San Jose, where her mother lived; that the confinement of office-work had threatened her with pulmonary tuberculosis (Andy failed, at the moment, to recognize the disease which had once threatened him also, and wondered vaguely) and that the doctor had advised her coming to Montana for a couple of months; that she had written to her father (it seemed queer to have anyone speak of old Take-Notice as "father") and that he had told her to "come a-running."

She told Andy that she had not seen her father for five years (Andy knew that Take-Notice had disappeared for a whole winter, about that long ago, and that no one had discovered where he went) because he and her mother were "not congenial."

He had dismounted, at her invitation, and had gone clanking to the doorstep and sat down—giving a furtive kick now and then at the black lamb, which developed a fondness for the leathern fringe on his chaps—and had eaten an orange which she had brought in her trunk all the way from San Jose, and which she had picked from a tree which stood by her mother's front gate. He had nibbled a ripe olive—eating it with what Andy himself would term "long teeth"—and had tried hard not to show how vile he found it. He had inspected two star-fishes which she had found last Fourth-of-July at Monterey and had dried; and had crumpled a withered leaf of bay in his hands and had smelled and nearly sneezed his head off; and had cracked and eaten four walnuts—also gathered from her mother's yard—and three almonds from the same source, and had stared admiringly at a note-book filled with funny marks which she called shorthand.

Between-whiles Andy had told her his name and the name of the outfit he worked for; had explained what he meant by "outfit," and had drawn a large U in the dirt to show her what a Flying U was, and had wanted to murder the black lamb which kept getting in his way and trying to eat the stick Andy used for a pencil; had confessed that he did sometimes play cards for money, as do the cowboys in Western stories, but assured her that he had never killed off any of his friends during any little disagreement. He had owned to drinking a glass of whisky now and then, but declared that it was only for snake bite and did not happen oftener than once in six months or so. Yes, he had often had rattlers in his bed, but not to hurt. This is where he began to inspect the star-fishes, and so turned the conversation safely back to California and himself away from the temptation to revel in fiction.

All of which took time, so that Take-Notice came before they quite felt a longing for his presence; and though the sun shone straight in the cabin door and so proved that it was full noon, there was no fire left in the stove and nothing in sight that was eatable save another ripe olive—which Andy had politely declined—and two more almonds and an orange.

A stenographer, with a fluffy pompadour that dipped distractingly at one side, and a gold watch suspended around the neck like a locket, and with sleeves that came no farther than the elbow and heels higher than any riding boot Andy ever owned in his life, and with teeth that were very white and showed a glint of gold here and there, and eyes that looked at one with insincere gravity, and fingers with nails that shone—fingers that pinched red lips together meditatively—a stenographer who has all these entrancing attributes, Andy discovered, may yet lack those housewifely accomplishments that make a man dream of a little home for two. So far as Andy could see, her knowledge of cookery extended no farther than rolled oat porridge for the two lambs.

Take-Notice it was who whittled shavings and started the fire without any comment upon the hour or his appetite; who went to the spring and brought water, half-filled the enameled teakettle which had large, bare patches where the enamel had been chipped off in the stress of baching, and sliced the bacon and mixed the "sour-dough" biscuits. To be sure, he had done those things for years and thought nothing of it; Andy, also, had done those things, many's the time, and had thought nothing of it, either. But to do them while a young woman sits calmly by and makes no offer of help, but talks of many things, unconscious even of her world-old, feminine duties and privileges, that struck Andy with a cold breath of disillusionment.

He watched her unobtrusively while she talked. She never once seemed to feel that cooking belonged to woman, and as far as he could see Take-Notice did not feel so either. So Andy mentally adjusted himself to the novelty and joyed in her presence.

To show how successful was his mental adjustment, it is necessary merely to state one fact: Where he had intended to stop an hour or so, he stayed the afternoon; ate supper there and rode home at sundown, his mind a jumble of sunny Californian days where one may gather star-fishes and oranges, bay leaves and ripe olives at will, and of black and white lambs which always obtrude themselves at the wrong moment and break off little, intimate confidences about life in a real-estate office, perhaps; and of polished finger-nails that never dip themselves in dishwater—Andy had come to believe that it would be neither right or just to expect them to do so common a thing.

The season was what the range calls "between roundups," so that Andy went straight to the ranch and found the Happy Family in or around the bunk-house, peacefully enjoying their before-bedtime smoke. Andy, among other positive faults and virtues, did not lack a certain degree of guile. Men there were at the Flying U who would ride in haste if they guessed that a pompadoured young woman from California was at the end of the trail, and Andy, knowing well the reputation he bore among them, set that reputation at work to keep the trail empty of all riders save himself. When someone asked him idly what had kept him so long, he gazed around at them with his big, innocent gray eyes.

"Why, I was just getting acquainted with the new girl," he answered simply and truthfully.

Truth being something which the Happy Family was unaccustomed to from the lips of Andy Green, they sniffed scornfully.

"What girl?" demanded Irish bluntly.

"Why, Take-Notice's girl. His young lady daughter that is visiting him. She's mighty nice, and she's got style about her, and she was feeding two lambs. Her name," he added softly, "is Mary."

Since no one had ever heard that Take-Notice had a daughter, the Happy Family could not be blamed for doubting Andy. They did doubt, profanely and volubly.

"Say, did any of you fellows ever eat a ripe olive?" Andy broke in, when he could make himself heard. "Well," he explained mildly, when came another rift of silence in the storm-cloud of words, "When yuh ride over there, she'll likely give yuh one to try; but yuh take my advice and pass it up. I went up against one, and I ain't got the taste out uh my mouth yet. It's sure fierce."

More words, from which Andy gathered that they did not believe anything he said; that he was wasting time and breath, and that his imagination was weak and his lies idiotic. He'd better not let Take-Notice hear how he was taking his name in vain and giving him a daughter—and so on.

"Say, did yuh ever see a star-fish? Funniest thing yuh ever saw, all pimply, and pink, and with five points to 'em. She's got two. When yuh go over, you ask her to let yuh see 'em." Andy was in bed, then, and he spoke through the dusk toward the voices. What those voices had just then been saying seemed to have absolutely no effect upon him.

"Oh, dry up!" Irish commanded impatiently. "Nobody's thinking uh riding over there, yuh chump. What kind of easy marks do yuh think we are?"

Andy laughed audibly in his corner next the window. "Say, you fellows do amuse me a lot. By gracious, I'll bet five dollars some of yuh take the trail over there, soon or late. I—I'll bet five dollars to *one* that yuh do! The bet to hold good for —well, say six weeks. But yuh better not take me up, boys—especially Irish, that ain't got a girl at present. Yes, or *any* of yuh, by gracious! It'll be a case for breach-uh-promise for any one uh yuh. Say, she's a bird! Got goldy hair, and a dimple in her chin and eyes that'd make a man—"

With much reviling they accepted the wager, and after that Andy went peacefully to sleep, quite satisfied for the time with the effect produced by his absolute truthfulness; it did not matter much, he told himself complacently, what a man's reputation might be, so long as he recognized its possibilities and shaped his actions properly.

It is true that when he returned from Dry Lake, not many days after, with a package containing four new ties and a large, lustrous silk handkerchief of the proper, creamy tint, the Happy Family seemed to waver a bit. When he took to shaving every other day, and became extremely fastidious about his finger-nails and his boots and the knot in his tie, and when he polished the rowels of his spurs with Patsy's scouring brick (which Patsy never used) and was careful to dent his hat-crown into four mathematically correct dimples before ever he would ride away from the ranch, the Happy Family looked thoughtful and discussed him privately in low tones.

But when Andy smilingly assured them that he was going over to call on Take-Notice's girl, and asked them if they wouldn't like to come along and be introduced, and taste a ripe olive, and look at the star-fishes, and smell a crumpled leaf of bay, they backed figuratively from the wiles of him and asserted more or less emphatically he couldn't work *them*. Then Andy would grin and ride gaily away, and Flying U Coulee would see him no more for several hours. It was mere good fortune—from Andy's viewpoint—that duty did not immediately call the Happy Family, singly or as a whole, to ride across the hills toward the cabin of Take-Notice Johnson. Without a legitimate excuse, he felt sure of their absence from the place, and he also counted optimistically upon their refusing to ask any one whom they might meet, if Take-Notice Johnson had a daughter visiting him.

Four weeks do not take much space in a calendar, nor much time to live; yet in the four that came just after Andy's discovery, he accomplished much, even in his own modest reckoning. He had taught the girl to watch for his coming and to stand pensively in the door with many good-bye messages when he said he must hit the trail. He had formed definite plans for the future and had promised her quite seriously that he would cut out gambling, and never touch liquor in any form—unless the snake was a *very* big one and sunk his fangs in a vital spot, in which dire contingency Mary absolved him from his vow. He had learned the funny marks that meant his name and hers in shorthand and had watched with inner satisfaction her efforts to learn how to fry canned corn in bacon grease, and to mix sour-dough biscuits that were neither yellow with too much soda nor distressfully "soggy" with too little, and had sat a whole, blissful afternoon in his shirtsleeves, while Mary bent her blond pompadour domestically over his coat, sewing in the sleeve-linings that are prone to come loose and torment a man. To go back to the first statement, which includes all these things and much more, Andy had, in those four weeks, accomplished much.

But a girl may not live forever in that lonely land with only Andy Green to discover her presence, and the rumors which at first buzzed unheeded in the ears of the Happy Family, stung them at last to the point of investigation; so that on a Sunday—the last Sunday before the Flying U wagons took again to the trailless range-land, Irish and Jack Bates rode surreptitiously up the coulee half an hour after Andy, blithe in his fancied security, had galloped that way to spend a long half-day with Mary. If he discovered them they would lose a dollar each—but if they discovered a girl such as Andy had pictured, they felt that it would be a dollar well lost.

In the range-land many strange things may happen. Irish and Jack pulled up short when, off to their right, in a particularly, lonely part of that country, broken into seamed coulees and deep-scarred hills, they heard a faint halloo. With spurs pricking deep and frequent they hurried to the spot; looked down a grassy swale and saw Andy lying full length upon the ground in rather a peculiar pose, while his horse fed calmly a rein-length away.

They stopped and looked at him, and at each other; rode cautiously to within easy rifle shot and stopped again.

"Ain't yuh getting tired feelings kinda unseasonable in the day?" Jack Bates called out guardedly.

"I—I'm hurt, boys," Andy lifted his head to say, strainedly. "My hoss stepped in a hole, and I wasn't looking for it. I guess—my leg's broke."

Jack snorted. "That so? Sure it ain't your neck, now? Seems to me your head sets kinda crooked. Better feel it and find out, while we go on where we're going." He half turned his horse up the hill again, resenting the impulse which had betrayed him a hand's breadth from the trail.

Andy waited a moment. Then: "On the dead, boys, my leg's broke—like you'd bust a dry stick. Come and see—for yourselves."

"Maybe—" Irish began, uncertainly, in an undertone. Andy's voice had in it a note of pain that was rather convincing.

"Aw, he's just trying to head us off. Didn't I help pack him up that ungodly bluff, last spring, thinking he was going to die before we got him to the top—and him riding off and giving us the horse-laugh to pay for it? You can bite, if yuh want to; I'm going on. I sure savvy Andy Green."

"Come and look," Andy begged from below. "If I'm joshing—"

"You can josh and be darned," finished Jack for him. "I don't pack you up hill more than once, old-timer. We're going to call on your Mary-girl. When yuh get good and refreshed up, you can come and look on at me and Irish acting pretty and getting a stand-in. So-long!"

Irish, looking back over his shoulder, saw Andy raise his head and gaze after them; saw it drop upon his arms just before they went quite over the hill. The sight stuck persistently and unpleasantly in his memory.

"Yuh know, he *might* be hurt," he began tentatively when they had ridden slowly a hundred yards or so.

"He might. But he ain't. He's up to some game again, and he wouldn't like anything better than to have us ride down there and feel his bones. If you'd been along, that day in the Bad-lands, you'd know the kind of bluff he can put up. Why, we all thought sure he was going to die. He acted that natural we felt like we was packing a corpse at a funeral—and him tickled to death all the while at the load he was throwing! No sir, yuh don't see me swallowing no such dope as *that*, any more. When he gets tired uh laying there, he'll recover rapid and come on. Don't yuh worry none about Andy Green; why, man, do yuh reckon any horse-critter could break *his* leg—a rider like him? He knows more ways uh falling off a horse without losing the ashes off his cigarette than most men know how to—how to punish grub! Andy Green *couldn't* get hurt with a horse! If he could, he'd uh been dead and playing his little harp long ago."

Such an argument was more convincing than the note of pain in the voice of Andy, so that Irish shook off his uneasiness and laughed at the narrow escape he'd had from being made a fool. And speedily they forgot the incident.

It was Take-Notice who made them remember, when they had been an hour or so basking themselves, so to speak, in the smiles of Mary. They had fancied all along that she had a curiously expectant air, and that she went very often to the door to see what the lambs were up to—and always lifted her eyes to the prairie slope down which they had ridden and gazed as long as she dared. They were not dull; they understood quite well what "lamb" it was that held half the mind of her, and they were piqued because of their understanding, and not disposed to further the cause of the absent. Therefore, when Take-Notice asked casually what had become of Andy, Jack Bates moved his feet impatiently, shot a sidelong glance at the girl (who was at that moment standing where she could look out of the window) and laughed unpleasantly.

"Oh, Andy's been took again with an attack uh bluff," he answered lightly. "He gets that way, ever so often, you know. We left him laying in a sunny spot, a few miles back, trying to make somebody think he was hurt, so they'd pack him home and he'd have the laugh on them for all summer."

"Wasn't he hurt?" The girl turned suddenly and her voice told how much it meant to her. But Jack was not sympathetic.

"No, he wasn't hurt. He was just playing off. He got us once, that way, and he's never given up the notion that he could do it again. We may be easy, but—"

"I don't understand," the girl broke in sharply. "Do you mean that he would deliberately try to deceive you into believing he was hurt, when he wasn't?"

"Miss Johnson," Jack replied sorrowfully, "he would. He would lose valuable sleep for a month, studying up the smoothest way to deceive. I guess," he added artfully, and as if the subject was nearly exhausted, "yuh don't know Mr. Green very well."

"I remember hearing about that job he put up on yuh," Take-Notice remarked, not noticing that the girl's lips were opened for speech, "Yuh made a stretcher, didn't yuh, and—"

"No—he told it that way, but he's such a liar he couldn't tell the truth if he wanted to. We found him lying at the bottom of a steep bluff, and he appeared to be about dead. It looked as if he'd slipped and fallen down part way. So we packed water and sloshed in his face, and he kinda come to, and then we packed him up the bluff—and yuh know what the Bad-lands is like, Take-Notice. It was unmerciful hot, too, and we like to died getting him up. At the top we laid him down and worked over him till we got him to open his eyes, and he could talk a little and said maybe he could ride if we could get him on a horse. The—he made us *lift* him into the saddle—and considering the size of him, it was something of a contract—and then he made as if he couldn't stay on, even. But first we knew he digs in the spurs, yanks off his hat and lets a yell out of him you could hear a mile, and says: 'Much obliged, boys, it was too blamed hot to walk up that hill,' and off he goes."

Take-Notice stretched his legs out before him, pushed his hands deep down in his trousers' pockets, and laughed and laughed. "That was sure one on you," he chuckled. "Andy's a hard case, all right."

But the girl stood before him, a little pale and with her chin high. "Father, how can you think it's funny?" she cried impatiently. "It seems to me—er—I think it's perfectly horrid for a man to act like that. And you say, Mr. Bates, that he's out there *now*"—she swept a very pretty hand and arm toward the window—"acting the same silly sort of falsehood?"

"I don't know where he is *now*," Jack answered judicially. "That's what he was doing when we came past."

She went to the door and stood looking vaguely out at nothing in particular, and Irish took the opportunity to kick Jack on the ankle-bone and viciously whisper, "Yuh damned chump!" But Jack smiled serenely. Irish, he reflected, had not been with them that day in the Bad-lands, and so had not the same cause for vengeance. He remembered that Irish had laughed, just as Take-Notice was laughing, when they told him about it; but Jack had never been able to see the joke, and his conscience did not trouble him now.

More they said about Andy Green—he and Take-Notice, with Irish mostly silent and with the girl extremely indignant at times and at others slightly incredulous, but always eager to hear more. More they said, not with malice, perhaps, for they liked Andy Green, but with the spirit of reminiscence strong upon them. Many things that he had said and done they recalled and laughed over—but the girl did not laugh. At sundown, when they rode away, she scribbled a hasty note, put it in an envelope and entrusted it to Irish for immediate delivery to the absent and erring one. Then they rode home, promising each other that they would sure devil Andy to death when they saw him, and wishing that they had ridden long ago to the cabin of Take-Notice. It was not pleasant to know that Andy Green had again fooled them completely.

None at the ranch had seen Andy, and they speculated much upon the nature of the game he was playing. Happy Jack wanted to bet that Andy really had broken his leg—but that was because he had a present grievance against Irish and hated to agree with anything he said. But when they went to bed, the Happy Family had settled unanimously upon the theory that Andy had ridden to Dry Lake, and would come loping serenely down the trail next day.

Irish did not know what time it was when he found himself sitting up in bed listening, but he discovered Pink getting quietly into his clothes. Irish hesitated a moment, and then felt under his pillow for his own garments—long habit had made him put them there—and began to dress. "I guess I'll go along with yuh," he whispered.

"Yuh can if yuh want to," Pink answered ungraciously. "But yuh needn't raise the long howl if—"

"Hold on, boys; my ante's on the table," came guardedly from Weary's bunk, and there was a soft, shuffling sound as of moving blankets; the subdued scrape of boots pulled from under bunks, and the quiet searching for hats and gloves. There was a clank of spur-chains, the faint squeal of a hinge gone rusty, a creak of a loose board, and then the three stood together outside under the star-sprinkle and avoided looking at one another. Without a word they went down the deep-worn path to the big gate, swung it open and headed for the corral where slept their horses.

"If them bone-heads don't wake up, nobody'll be any the wiser—and it's a lovely night for a ramble," murmured Weary, consoling himself.

"Well, I couldn't sleep," Irish confessed, half defiantly. "I expect it's just a big josh, but—it won't do any hurt to make sure."

"Yuh all think Andy Green lives to tell lies," snapped Pink, throwing the saddle on his horse with a grunt at the weight of it. The horse flinched away from its impact, and Pink swore at it viciously. "Yuh might uh gone down and made sure, anyhow," he criticised.

"Well, I was going to; but Jack said—" Irish stooped to pick up the latigo and did not finish. "But I can't get over the way his head dropped down on his arms, when we were riding out uh sight. As if—oh, hell! If it was a josh, I'll just about beat the head off him for spoiling my sleep this way. Get your foot off that rein, yuh damned, clumsy bench!" This last to his horse.

They rode slowly away from the ranch and made the greater haste when the sound of their galloping could not reach the dulled ears of those who slept. They did not talk much, and when they did it was to tell one another what great fools they were—but even in the telling they urged their horses to greater speed.

"Well," Pink summed up at last, "if he's hurt, out here, we're doing the right thing; and if he ain't, he won't be there to have the laugh on us; so it's all right either way."

There was black shadow in the grassy swale where they found him. His horse had wandered off and it was only the sure instinct of Irish that led them to the spot where he lay, a blacker shadow in the darkness that a passing cloud had made. Just at first they thought him dead, but when they lifted him he groaned and then spoke.

"It's one on me, this time," he said, and the throat of Irish pinched achingly together at the sound of his voice, which had in it the note of pain he had been trying to forget.

After that he said nothing at all, because he was a senseless weight in their arms.

At daylight Irish was pounding vehemently the door of the White House and calling for the Little Doctor. Andy lay stretched unconscious upon the porch beside him, and down in the bunk-house the Happy Family was rubbing eyes and exclaiming profanely at the story Pink was telling.

"And here," finished Irish a couple of hours later, when he was talking the thing over with the Little Doctor, "here's a note Take-Notice's girl gave me for him. I don't reckon there's any good news in it, so maybe yuh better hold it out on him till he's got over the fever. I guess we queered Andy a lot—but I'll ride over, soon as I can, and fix it up with her and tell her he broke his leg, all right. Maybe," he finished optimistically, "she'll come over to see him."

Irish kept his word, though he delayed until the next day; and the next day it was too late. For the cabin of Take-Notice was closed and empty, and the black lamb and the white were nosing unhappily their over-turned pan of mush, and bleating lonesomely. Irish waited a while and started home again; rode into the trail and met Bert Rogers, who explained:

"Take-Notice was hauling his girl, trunk and all, to the depot," he told Irish. "I met 'em just this side the lane. They aimed to catch the afternoon train, I reckon. She was going home, Take-Notice told me."

So Irish rode thoughtfully back to the ranch and went straight to the White House where Andy lay, meaning to break the news as carefully as he knew how.

Andy was lying in bed looking big-eyed at the ceiling, and in his hand was the note. He turned his head and glanced indifferently at Irish.

"Yuh sure made a good job of it, didn't yuh?" he began calmly, though it was not the calm which meant peace. "I was just about engaged to that girl. If it'll do yuh any good to know how nice and thorough yuh busted everything up for me, read that." He held out the paper, and Irish turned a guilty red when he took it.

"Mr. Green: I have just been greatly entertained with the history of your very peculiar deeds and adventures, and I wish to say that I have discovered myself wholly lacking the sense of humor which is necessary to appreciate you.

"As I am going home to-morrow, this is my only opportunity of letting you know how thoroughly I detest falsehood in *any* form. Yours truly,

"MARY EDITH JOHNSON."

"Ain't yuh proud?" Andy inquired in a peculiar, tired voice. "Maybe I'm a horrible liar, all right—but I never done anybody a dirty trick like that."

Irish might have said it was Jack Bates who did the mischief, but he did not. "We never knew it was anything serious," he explained contritely. "On the dead, I'm sorry—"

"And that does a damned lot uh good—if she's gone!" Andy cut in, miserably.

"Oh, she's gone, all right. She went to-day," murmured Irish, and went out and shut the door softly behind him.

FOOL'S GOLD.

Andy Green, unshaven as to face and haggard as to eyes, leaned upon his stout, willow stick and looked gloomily away to the west. He was a good deal given to looking to the west, these days when a leg new-healed kept him at the ranch, though habit and inclination would have sent him riding fast and far over prairies untamed. Inaction comes hard when a man has lived his life mostly in the open, doing those things which keep brain and muscle keyed alike to alertness and leave no time for brooding.

If Andy had not broken his leg but had gone with the others on roundup, he would never have spent the days glooming unavailingly because a girl with a blond pompadour and teasing eyes had gone away and taken with her a false impression of his morals, and left behind her the sting of a harsh judgment against which there seemed no appeal. As it was, he spent the time going carefully over his past in self-justification, and in remembering every moment that he had spent with Mary Johnson in those four weeks when she stayed with her father and petted the black lamb and the white.

In his prejudiced view, he had never done anything to make a girl hate him. He had not always told the truth—he would admit that with candid, gray eyes looking straight into your own—but he had never lied to harm a man, which, it seemed to him, makes all the difference in the world.

If he could once have told her how he felt about it, and showed her how the wide West breeds wider morals—he did not quite know how you would put these things, but he felt them very keenly. He wanted to make her feel the difference; to see that little things do not count in a man's life, after all, except when they affect him as a man when big things are wanted of him. A little cowardice would count, for instance, because it would show that the man would fail at the test; but a little lie? just a harmless sort of lie that was only a "josh" and was taken as such by one's fellows? Andy was not analytic by nature, and he would have stumbled vaguely among words to explain his views, but he felt very strongly the injustice of the girl's condemnation, and he would scarcely speak to Jack Bates and Irish when they came around making overtures for peace and goodwill.

"If she hadn't gone home so sudden, I could uh squared it all right," he told the Little Doctor, whenever her sympathetic attitude won him to speech upon the subject.

"Yes, I believe you could," she would agree cheeringly. "If she's the right sort, and cared, you could."

"She's the right sort—I know that," Andy would assert with much decision, though modesty forbade his telling the Little Doctor that he was also sure she cared. She did care, if a girl's actions count for anything, or her looks and smiles. Of course she cared! Else why did she rush off home like that, a good month before she had intended to go? They had planned that Andy would get a "lay-off" and go with her as far as Butte, because she would have to wait there several hours, and Andy wanted to take her out to the Columbia Gardens and see if she didn't think they were almost as nice as anything California could show. Then she had gone off without any warning because Jack Bates and Irish had told her a lot of stuff about him, Andy; if that didn't prove she cared, argued Andy to himself, what the dickens would you want for proof?

It was from thinking these things over and over while he lay in bed, that Andy formed the habit of looking often towards the west when his hurt permitted him to hobble around the house. And when a man looks often enough in any direction, his feet will, unless hindered by fate itself, surely follow his gaze if you give them time enough.

It was the excursion rates advertised in a Great Falls paper that first put the idea consciously into the brain of Andy. They seemed very cheap, and the time-limit was generous, and—San Jose was not very far from San Francisco, the place named in the advertisement; and if he could only see the girl and explain—It would be another month before he would be able to work, anyway, and—A man might as well get rid of a hundred or so travelling, as to sit in a poker game and watch it fade away, and he would really get more out of it. Anyhow, nobody need know where he had gone. They could think he was just going to Butte. And he didn't give a darn if they did find it out!

He limped back into the house and began inspecting, with much dissatisfaction, his wardrobe. He would have to stake himself to new clothes—but he needed clothes, anyway, that fall. He could get what he wanted in Butte, while he waited for the train to Ogden. Now that Andy had made up his mind to go, he was in a great hurry and grudged the days, even the hours, that must pass before he could see Mary Edith Johnson.

Not even the Little Doctor knew the truth, when Andy appeared next morning dressed for his journey, ate a hasty and unsatisfactory breakfast and took the Old Man to one side with elaborate carelessness and asked for a sum that made the Old Man blink. But no man might have charge of the Happy Family for long without attaining that state of mental insulation which renders a shock scientifically impossible. The Old Man wrote a check, twisted his mouth into a whimsical knot and inquired mildly: "What's the brand of devilment this time, and how long's it going to take yuh?" With a perceptible emphasis on the word *this*.

For probably the first time in his life Andy blushed and stammered over a lie, and before he had got out more than two words, the Old Man seemed to understand the situation quite thoroughly. He said "Oh, I see. Well, git a round-trip ticket and be dead sure yuh don't out-stay the limit." He took out his pipe and filled it meditatively.

Andy blushed again—six weeks indoors had lightened the tan on his face so that his blushes showed very plainly—and made desperate denial. "I'm only going up to Butte. But a fellow can't have any kind of a time there without a fair-sized roll, and—I'll be back in two or three weeks—soon as my leg's mended thorough. I—"

"Get along with yuh!" growled the Old Man, though his eyes twinkled. "Doggone it, don't yuh lie to *me*. Think I was shipped in on the last train? A man don't git red in the face when he's just merely headed for Butte. Why, doggone yuh—"

The last words had to serve for a farewell, because Andy was limping away as fast as he could, and did not come back to the house again. He did not even tell the Little Doctor good-by, though it was fifteen minutes before John Wedum, the ranchhand, had the team ready to drive Andy to town, and he was one of the Little Doctor's most loyal subjects.

Andy walked haltingly down a palm-shaded street in San Jose and wondered just what would be the best and quickest way in which to find Mary Edith Johnson. Three ways were open to him: He could hunt up all the Johnsons in town—there were three full pages of them in the directory, as he remembered with a sigh—and find out which one was the right one; but San Jose, as he had already discovered, was not a village, and he doubted if he could stand the walking. He could visit all the real estate offices in town—and he was just beginning to realize that there were almost as many real estate offices as there were Johnsons. And he could promenade the streets in the hope of meeting her. But always there was the important fact to face—the fact that San Jose is not a village.

He came upon a particularly shady spot and a bench placed invitingly. Andy sat down, eased the new-healed leg out before him and rolled a cigarette. "This is going to be some different from hunting a stray on the range," he told himself, with an air of deliberate cheerfulness. "If I could get out and scurrup around on a hoss, and round her up that way—but this footing it all over town is what grinds me." He drew a match along the under side of the bench and held the blaze absently to the cigarette. "There was one thing—she told about an orange tree right beside her mother's front gate, Maybe—" He looked around him hopefully. Just across the street was a front gate, and beside it an orange tree; he knew because there were ripe oranges hanging upon it. He started to rise, his blood jumping queerly, sat down again and swore. "Every darned gate in town, just about, has got an orange tree stuck somewhere handy by. I remember 'em now, damn 'em!"

Three cigarettes he smoked while he sat there. When he started on again his face was grimly set toward the nearest business street. At the first real-estate sign he stopped, pulled together his courage, and went in. A girl sat in a corner of the room before a typewriter. Andy saw at a glance that her hair was too dark; murmured something and backed out. At the next place, a man was crumpled into a big chair, reading a paper. Behind a high desk a typewriter clicked, but Andy could not see the operator without going behind the railing, and he hesitated.

"Looking for a snap?" asked the man briskly, coming up from his crumpled state like a spring.

"Well, I was looking—"

"Now, here. It may not be what you want, but I'm just going to show you this proposition and see what you think of it. It ain't going to last—somebody's goin' to snap it up before you know it. Now, here—"

It was half an hour before Andy got away from that office, and he had not seen who was running the machine behind the desk, even then. He had, however, spoken rather loudly and had informed the man that he was from Montana, with no effect whatever upon the clicking. He had listened patiently to the glowing description of several "good buys," and had escaped with difficulty within ten minutes after hearing the unseen typist addressed as "Fern."

At the third place he merely looked in at the door and retreated hastily when the agent, like a spider on the watch, started forward.

When he limped into the office of his hotel at six o'clock, Andy was ready to swear that every foot of land in California was for sale, and that every man in San Jose was trying his best to sell it and looked upon him, Andy Green, as a weak-minded millionaire who might be induced to purchase. He had not visited all the places where they kept bulletin-boards covered with yellowed placards abounding in large type and many fat exclamation points and the word ONLY with a dollar mark immediately after. All? He had not visited half of them, or a third!

That night he dreamed feverishly of "five-room, modern cottages with bath," and of ONLY $500.00 down and balance payable monthly," and of ten-acre "ranches" and five-acre "ranches"—he who had been used to numbering acres by the thousand and to whom the word "ranch" meant miles of wire fencing and beyond that miles of open!

It took all the longing he felt for Mary Johnson to drive him out the next morning and to turn his face toward those placarded places which infested every street, but he went. He went with eyes that glared hostility at every man who said "buy," and with chin set to stubborn purpose. He meant to find Mary Edith Johnson, and he meant to find her without all California knowing that he was looking for her. Not once had he mentioned her name, or showed that he cared whether there was a typewriter in the office or whether it was a girl, man or Chinaman who clicked the keys; and yet he knew exactly how every girl typist had her hair dressed, and what was the color of her eyes.

At two o'clock, Andy stopped suddenly and stared down at a crack in the pavement, and his lips moved in muttered speech. "She's worked three years in one of them places—and she 'thoroughly detests falsehood in *any* form'! Hell!" Is exactly what he was saying out loud, on one of the busiest streets in San Jose.

A policeman glanced at him, looked again and came slowly toward him. Andy took the hint and moved on decorously to the next bulletin-board, but the revelation that had come to him there in the street dulled somewhat his alertness, so that he came near committing himself to the purchase of one of those ubiquitous "five-room, modern cottages with bath" before he realized what he was doing and fled to the street again, on the pretense that he had to catch the car which was just slowing down for that crossing.

He boarded the car, though he had no idea of where it was going, and fished in his pocket for a nickel. And just when he was reaching up from the step where he stood clinging—reaching over the flower-piled hat of a girl, to place the nickel in the outstretched palm of the conductor, he heard for the first time in many weeks the name of Mary Johnson. A girl at his elbow was asking the other: "What'n the world's become of Mary Johnson? She wasn't to the dance last night, and it's the first one—"

Andy held his breath.

"Oh, Mame quit her place with Kelly and Gray, two weeks ago. She's gone to Santa Cruz and got a place for the summer. Her and Lola Parsons went together, and—"

Andy took advantage of another crossing, and dropped off. He wanted to find out when the next train left for Santa Cruz. It never occurred to him that there might be two Mary Johnsons in the world, which was fortunate, perhaps; he wasted no time in hesitation, and so, within twenty minutes, he was hearing the wheels of a fast train go *clickety-click, clickety-click* over the switches in the suburbs of San Jose, and he was asking the conductor what time the train would reach Santa Cruz, and was getting snubbed for his anxiety.

Santa Cruz, when he did reach it, seemed, on a superficial examination, to be almost as large as San Jose, and the real-estate offices closer together and even more plentifully supplied with modern cottages and bath—and the heart of him sank prophetically. For the first time since he dropped off the street-car in San Jose, it seemed to him that Mary Johnson was quite as far off, quite as unattainable as she had ever been.

He walked slowly up Pacific Avenue and watched the hurrying crowds, and wondered if chance would be kind to him; if he should meet her on the street, perhaps. He did not want to canvass all the real-estate offices in town. "It would take me till snow flies," he murmured dispiritedly, forgetting that here was a place where snow never flew, and sought a hotel where they were not "full to the eaves" as two complacent clerks had already told him.

At supper, he made friends with a genial-voiced insurance agent—the kind who does not insist upon insuring your life whether you want it insured or not. The agent told Andy to call him Jack and use him good and plenty—perhaps because something wistful and lonely in the gray eyes of Andy appealed to him—and Andy took him at his word and was grateful. He discovered what day of the week it was: Saturday, and that on the next day Santa Cruz would be "wide-open" because of an excursion from Sacramento. Jack offered to help him lose himself in the crowd, and again Andy was grateful. For the first time since leaving the Flying U he went to bed feeling not utterly alone and friendless, and awoke pleasantly expectant. Friend Jack was to pilot him down to the Casino at eleven, and he had incidentally made one prediction which stuck closely to Andy, even in his sleep. Jack had assured him that the whole town would be at the beach; and if the whole town were at the beach, why then, Mary would surely be somewhere in the crowd. And if she were in the crowd—"If she's there, I'll sure get a line on her before night," Andy told himself, with much assurance. "A fellow that's been in the habit of cutting any certain brand of critter out of a big herd ought to be able to spot his girl in a crowd"—and he hummed softly while he dressed.

The excursion train was already in town, and the esplanade was, looking down from Beach Hill, a slow-moving river of hats, with splotches of bright colors and with an outer fringe of men and women. "That's a good-sized trail-herd uh humans," Andy remarked, and the insurance agent laughed appreciatively.

"You wait till you see them milling around on the board walk," he advised impressively. "If you happen to be looking for anybody, you'll realize that there's some people scattered around in your vicinity. I had a date with a girl, down here one Sunday during the season, and we hunted each other from ten in the morning till ten at night and never got sight of each other."

Andy gave him a sidelong, suspicious glance, but friend Jack was evidently as innocent as he looked, and so Andy limped silently down the hill to the Casino and wondered if fate were going to cheat him at the last moment.

Once in the crowd, it was as Jack had told him it would be. He could not regard the moving mass of humanity as individuals, though long living where men are few had fixed upon him the habit. Now, although he observed far more than did Jack, he felt somewhat at a loss; the realization that Mary Johnson might pass him unrecognized troubled him greatly. It did not once occur to him that he, with his gray Stetson hat and his brown face and keen eyes and tall, straight-backed figure, looked not at all like the thousands of men all around him, so that many eyes turned to give him another glance when he passed. Mary Johnson must be unobserving in the extreme if she failed to know him, once she glimpsed him in the crowd.

Somewhere near one o'clock he lost Jack completely, and drifted aimlessly alone. Jack had been hailed by a friend, had stopped for a minute to talk, and several hundred men, women and children had come between him and Andy, pushing and crowding and surging, because a band had started playing somewhere. Andy got down the steps and out upon the sand, and Jack was thereafter but a memory. He found the loose sand hard walking with his lame leg, and almost as crowded as the promenade, and as he stood for a minute looking up at the board walk above him, it occurred to him that if he could get somewhere and stay there long enough, every human being at the Casino would eventually pass by him. He went up the steps again and worked his way along the edge of the walk until he found a vacant spot on the railing and sat grimly down upon it to wait.

Many cigarettes he smoked while he roosted there, watching until the eyes of him ached with the eternal panorama of faces that were strange. Many times he started eagerly because he glimpsed a fluffy, blond pompadour with blue eyes beneath, and fancied for an instant that it was Mary.

Then, when he was speculating upon the advisability of following the stream of people that flowed out upon the pleasure pier, Mary passed by so close that her skirt brushed his toes; passed him by, and he sat there like a paralytic and let her go. And in the heart of him was a queer, heavy throb that he did not in the least understand.

She was dressed in blue linen with heavy, white lace in patches here and there, and she had a big, white hat tilted back from her face and a long white plume drooping to one shoulder. Another girl was with her, and a man—a man with dented panama hat and pink cheeks and a white waistcoat and tan shoes; a man whom Andy suddenly hated most unreasonably.

When they were all but lost in the crowd, Andy got down, gripped his cane vindictively and followed. After all, the man was walking beside the other girl, and not beside Mary—and the reflection brought much solace. With the nodding, white feather to guide him, he followed them down the walk, lost them for a second, saw them turn in at the wide-open doors of the natatorium, saw them pause there, just inside. Then a huge woman pushed before him, stood there and narrowed his range of vision down to her own generous hat with its huge roses, and when he had edged past her the three were gone.

Andy waited, comforted by the knowledge that they had not come out, until the minutes passed his patience and he went in, searched the gallery unavailingly, came out again and wandered on dispiritedly to the pleasure pier. There, leaning over the rail, he saw her again almost beneath him in the sand, scantily clad in a bathing suit. The man, still more scantily clad, was trying to coax her into the water and she was hanging back and laughing a good deal, with an occasional squeal.

Andy leaned rather heavily upon the railing and watched her gloweringly, incredulously. Custom has much to do with a man's (or a woman's) idea of propriety, and one Andrew Green had for long been unaccustomed to the sight of nice young women disporting themselves thus in so public a place. He could not reconcile it with the girl as he had known her in her father's cabin, and he was not at all sure that he wanted to do so.

He was just turning gloomily away when she glanced up, saw him and waved her hand. "Hello, Andy," she called gaily. "Come on down and take a swim, why don't you?"

Andy, looking reproachfully into her upturned face, shook his head. "I can't," he told her. "I'm lame yet." It was not at all what he had meant to say, any more than this was the meeting he had dreamed about. He resented both with inner rage.

"Oh. When did you come?" she asked casually, and was whisked away by the man before Andy could tell her. The other girl was there also, and the three ran gleefully down to meet a roller larger than the others had been; met it, were washed, with much screaming and laughter, back to shore and stood there dripping. Andy glared down upon them and longed for the privilege of drowning the fellow.

"We're going up into the plunge," called Mary. "Come on. I'll see you, when I come out." They scampered away, and he, calling himself many kinds of fool, followed.

In the plunge, Andy was still more at a disadvantage, for since he was a spectator, a huge sign informed him that he must go up stairs. He went up with much difficulty into the gallery, found himself a seat next the rail and searched long for Mary among the bathers below. He would never have believed that he would fail to know her at sight, but with fifty women, more or less, dressed exactly alike and with ugly rubber caps pulled down to eyebrows and ears, recognition must necessarily be slow.

While he leaned and stared, an avalanche of squeals came precipitately down the great slide; struck the water and was transformed to gurgling screams, and then heads came bobbing to the surface — three heads, and one of them was Mary's. She swept the water from her eyes, looked up and saw him, waved her hand and scrambled rather ungracefully over the rail in her wet, clinging suit. The others followed, the man trotting at her heels and calling something after her.

Andy, his brows pulled down over unhappy eyes, glared fixedly up at the top of the slide. In a minute they appeared, held gesticulating counsel, wavered and came down together, upon their stomachs. The strange girl was in the lead, with Mary next holding to the girl's feet. Behind her slid the man, gripping tightly the ankles of Mary. Andy's teeth set savagely together, though he saw that others were doing exactly the same; old women, young women, girls, men and boys came hurtling down the big slide, singly, in couples, in three and fours.

The spectacle began to fascinate him, so that for a minute or two he could forget Mary and the man. There was a roar of voices, the barking as of seals, screams, laughter and much splashing. Men and women dove from the sides like startled frogs into a pond; they swam, floated and stood panting along the walls; swung from the trapeze (Andy, remembering his career with the circus, when he was "André de Gréno," Champion Bareback Rider of the Western Hemisphere, wished that his leg was well so that he could show them a few things about that trapeze business) and troubled the waters with much splashing. He could not keep Mary always in view, but when he did get sight of her she seemed to be having a very good time, and not to be worrying in the least about him and his sins.

Twice Andy Green half rose from his seat, meaning to leave the plunge, the Casino and the whole merry-making crowd; but each time he settled back, telling himself that he hated a quitter, and that he guessed he'd buy a few more chips and stay in the game.

It seemed a long time before Mary finally emerged in the blue linen and the white hat, but Andy was waiting doggedly at the entrance and took his place beside her, forcing the man to walk beside the girl whom Mary introduced as Lola Parsons. The man's name was Roberts, but the girls called him Freddie, and he seemed composed mostly of a self-satisfied smile and the latest fad in male attire. Andy set himself to the task of "cutting Mary out of the main herd" so that he might talk with her. Thus it happened that, failing a secluded spot in the immediate neighborhood of the Casino, which buzzed like a disturbed hive of gigantic bees, Mary presently found herself on a car that was clanging its signal of departure, and there was no sign of Freddie and Lola Parsons.

"We lost 'em, back there," Andy told her calmly when she inquired. "And as to where we're going, I don't know; as far as this lightning-wagon will take us."

"This car goes clear out to the Cliffs," Mary said discouragingly.

"All right. We're going out to the cliffs, then," Andy smiled blandly down upon the nodding, white feather in her hat.

"But I promised Lola and Freddie—"

"Oh, that's all right. I'll take the blame. Were yuh surprised to see me here?"

"Why should I be? Everybody comes to Santa Cruz, sooner or later."

"I came sooner," said Andy, trying to meet her eye. He wanted to bring the conversation to themselves, so that he might explain and justify himself, and win forgiveness for his sins.

While they walked along the cliffs he tried, and going home he had not given up the attempt. But afterward, when he could sit down quietly and think, he was forced to admit that he had not succeeded very well. It seemed to him that, while Mary still liked him and was quite ready to be friends, she had forgotten just why she had so suddenly left Montana. She was sorry he had broken his leg, but in the same breath, almost, she told him of such a narrow escape that Freddie had last week, when an auto nearly ran him down. Andy regretted keenly that it had not.

He had mentioned Irish and Jack Bates, meaning to refute the tales they had told of him, and she had asked about the black lamb and the white, and then had told him that he must go out to the whistling buoy and see the real whale they had anchored out there, and related with much detail how Freddie had taken her and Lola out, and how the water was so rough she got seasick, and a wave splashed over and ruined Freddie's new summer suit, that spotted dreadfully; it wasn't, she remarked, a durable color. She hoped Andy would stay a month or two, though the "season" was about over. She knew he would just love the plunge and the surf-bathing, and there was going to be a boomers' barbacue up at the Big Trees in two weeks—and it would seem like home to him, seeing a cow roasted whole! She did love Montana, and she hoped he brought his chaps and spurs along, for she had told Lola so much about him, and she wanted Lola to see him in his Wild West clothes.

All this should have pleased Andy very much. She had not grown cold, and her eyes were quite as teasing and her smiles as luring as before. She did not even lay personal claim to Freddie, that he should be jealous. When she spoke of Freddie, his name was linked with Lola Parsons, and Andy could not glean that she had ever gone anywhere alone with him. She had seemed anxious that he should enjoy his vacation to the limit, and had mentioned three or four places that he must surely see, and informed him three times that she was "off" at five every evening, and could show him around.

They had dined together at a café, and had gone back to the Casino for the band concert, and they had not been interrupted by meeting Lola Parsons and

Freddie, and she had given him a very cordial good-night when they parted on the steps of her boarding house at eleven.

So there was absolutely no reason for the mood Andy was in when he accepted his key from the hotel clerk and went up to his room. For a man who has traveled more than a thousand miles in search of the girl he had dreamed of o'nights, and who had found her and had been properly welcomed, he was distinctly gloomy. He sat down by the open window and smoked four cigarettes, said "Damn Freddy!" three times and with added emphasis each time, though he knew very well that Freddie had nothing to do with it, and then went to bed.

In the morning he felt better, and went out by himself to the cliffs where they had been before, and sat down on a hummock covered with short grass, and watched the great unrest of the ocean, and wondered where the Flying U wagons would be camping, that night. Somehow, the wide reach of water reminded him of the prairie; the rolling billows were like many, many cattle milling restlessly in a vast herd and tossing white heads and horns upward. Below him, the pounding surf was to him the bellowing of a thirsty herd corralled.

"This is sure all right," he approved, rousing a little. "It's almost as good as sitting up on a pinnacle and looking out over the range. If I had a good hoss, and my riding outfit, and could get out there and go to work cutting-out them white-caps and hazing 'em up here on a run, it wouldn't be so poor. By gracious, this is worth the trip, all right." It never occurred to Andy that there was anything strange in the remark, or that he sat there because it dulled the heavy ache that had been his since yesterday—the ache of finding what he had sought, and finding with it disillusionment.

Till hunger drove him away he stayed, and his dreams were of the wide land he had left. When he again walked down Pacific Avenue the hall clock struck four, and after he had eaten he looked up at it and saw that it lacked but fifteen minutes of five.

"I'm supposed to meet her when she quits work," he remembered, "and Lola and Freddie will go to the plunge with us." He stopped and stared in at the window of a curio store. "Say, that's a dandy Navajo blanket," he murmured. "It would be out-uh-sight for a saddle blanket." He started on, hesitated and went back. "I've got time enough to get it," he explained to himself. He went in, bought the blanket and two Mexican *serapes* that caught his fancy, tucked the bundle under his arm and started down the street toward the office where Mary worked. It was just two minutes *to five*.

He got almost to the door—so near that his toe struck against a corner of the belabelled bulletin board—when a sudden revulsion swept his desires back like a huge wave. He stood a second irresolutely and then turned back. "Aw—hell! What's the use?" he muttered.

The clock was just on the last stroke of five when he went up to the clerk in his hotel. "Say, when does the next train pull out?—I don't give a darn in what direction," he wanted to know. When the clerk told him seven-thirty, he grinned and became undignifiedly loquacious.

"I want to show yuh a couple of dandy *serapes* I just glommed, down street," he said, and rolled the bundle open upon the desk. "Ain't they a couple uh beauts? I got 'em for two uh my friends; they done me a big favor, a month or two ago, and I wanted to kinda square the deal. That's why I got 'em just alike. Yes, you bet they're peaches; yuh can't get 'em like this in Montana. The boys'll sure appreciate 'em." He retied the bundle, took his room-key from the hand of the smiling clerk and started up the stairway, humming a tune under his breath as he went.

At the first turn he stopped and looked back. "Send the bell-hop up to wake me at seven," he called down to the clerk. "I'm going to take a much-needed nap— and it'll be all your life's worth to let me miss that train!"

LORDS OF THE POTS AND PANS

The camp of the Flying U, snuggled just within the wide-flung arms of an unnamed coulee with a pebbly-bottomed creek running across its front, looked picturesque and peaceful—from a distance. Disenchantment lay in wait for him who strayed close enough to hear the wrangling in the cook-tent, however, or who followed Slim to where he slumped bulkily down into the shade of a willow fifty yards or so from camp—a willow where Pink, Weary, Andy Green and Irish were lying sprawled and smoking comfortably.

Slim grunted and moved away from a grass-hidden rock that was gouging him in the back. "By golly, things is getting pretty raw around this camp," he growled, by way of lifting the safety-valve of his anger. "I'd like to know when that darned grub-spoiler bought into the outfit, anyhow. He's been trying to run it to suit himself all spring—and if he keeps on, by golly, he'll be firing the wagon-boss and giving all the orders himself!"

It would seem that sympathy should be offered him; as if the pause he made plainly hinted that it was expected. Andy Green rolled over and sent him a friend-ly glance just to hearten him a bit.

"We were listening to the noise of battle," he observed, "and we were going over, in a minute, to carry off the dead. You had a kinda animated discussion over something, didn't yuh?" Andy was on his good behavior, as he had been for a month. His treatment of his fellows lately was little short of angelic. His tone soothed Slim to the point where he could voice his woe.

"Well, by golly, I guess he knows what I think of him, or pretty near. I've stood a lot from Patsy, off and on, and I've took just about all I'm going to. It's got so yuh can't get nothing to eat, hardly, when yuh ride in late, unless yuh fight for it. Why, by golly, I caught him just as he was going to empty out the coffee-boiler—and he knew blamed well I hadn't eat. He'd left everything go cold, and he was packing away the grub like he was late breaking camp and had a forty mile drive before dinner, by golly! I just did save myself some coffee, and that was all—but it was cold as that creek, and—" Habit impelled him to stop there long enough to run his tongue along the edge of a half-rolled cigarette, and accident caused his eyes to catch the amused quirk on the lips of Pink and Irish, and the laughing glance they exchanged. Possibly if he could have looked in all directions at the same time he would have been able to detect signs of mirth on the faces of the others as well; for Slim's grievances never seemed to be taken seriously by his companions—which is the price which one must pay for having a body shaped like Santa Claus and a face copied after our old friend in the moon.

"Well, by golly, maybe it's funny—but I took notice yuh done some yowling, both uh yuh, the other day when yuh didn't get no pie," he snorted, lighting his cigarette with unsteady fingers.

"We wasn't laughing at that," lied Pink pacifically.

"And then, by golly, the old devil lied to me and said there wasn't no pie left," went on Slim complainingly, his memory stirred by the taunt he had himself given. "But I wouldn't take his word for a thing if I knew it was so; I went on a still-hunt around that tent on my own hook, and I found a pie—a *whole pie*, by golly!—cached away under an empty flour-sack behind the stove! That," he added, staring, round-eyed, at the group, "that there was right where me and Patsy mixed. The lying old devil said he never knew a thing about it being there at all."

Pink turned his head cautiously so that his eyes met the eyes of Andy Green. The two had been at some pains to place that pie in a safe place so that they might be sure of something appetizing when they came in from standing guard that night, but neither seemed to think it necessary to proclaim the fact and clear Patsy.

"I'll bet yuh didn't do a thing to the pie when yuh did find it?" Pink half questioned, more anxious than he would have owned.

"By golly, I eat the whole thing and I cussed Patsy between every mouthful!" boasted Slim, almost in a good-humor again. "I sure got the old boy stirred up; I left him swearin' Dutch cuss-words that sounded like he was peevish. But I'll betche he won't throw out the coffee till I've had what I want after this, by golly!"

"Happy Jack is out yet," Weary observed after a sympathetic silence. "You oughtn't to have put Patsy on the fight till everybody was filled up, Slim. Happy's liable to go to bed with an empty tummy, if yuh don't ride out and warn him to approach easy. Listen over there!"

From where they lay, so still was the air and so incensed was Patsy, they could hear plainly the rumbling of his wrath while he talked to himself over the dish-washing. When he appeared at the corner of the tent or plodded out toward the front of the wagon, his heavy tread and stiff neck proclaimed eloquently the mood he was in. They watched and listened and were secretly rather glad they were fed and so need not face the storm which Slim had raised; for Patsy thoroughly roused was very much like an angry bull: till his rage cooled he would charge whoever approached him, absolutely blind to consequences.

"Well, I ain't going to put nobody next," Slim asserted. "Happy's got to take chances, same as I did. And while we're on the subject, Patsy was on the prod before I struck camp, or he wouldn't uh acted the way he done. Somebody else riled him up, by golly—I never."

"Well, you sure did put the finishing touches to him," contended Irish, guiltily aware that he himself was originally responsible; for Patsy never had liked Irish very well because of certain incidents connected with his introduction to Weary's double. Patsy never could quite forget, though he might forgive, and resentment lay always close to the surface of his mood when Irish was near.

Happy Jack, hungry and quite unconscious that he was riding straight into the trail of trouble, galloped around a ragged point of service-berry bushes, stopped with a lurch at the prostrate corral and unsaddled hastily. Those in the shade of the willow watched him, their very silence proclaiming loudly their interest. They might have warned him by a word, but they did not; for Happy Jack was never eager to heed warnings or to take advice, preferring always to abide by the rule of opposites. Stiff-legged from long riding, the knees of his old, leather chaps bulging out in transient simulation of bowed limbs, he came clanking down upon the cook-tent with no thought but to ease his hunger.

Those who watched saw him stoop and thrust his head into the tent, heard a bellow and saw him back out hastily. They chuckled unfeelingly and strained ears to miss no word of what would follow.

"Aw, gwan!" Happy Jack expostulated, not yet angry. "I got here quick as I could—and *I* ain't heard nothing about no new laws uh getting here when the whistle blows. Gimme what there is, anyhow."

Some sentences followed which, because of guttural tones and German accent emphasized by excitement, were not quite coherent to the listeners. However, they did not feel at all mystified as to his meaning—knowing Patsy as they did.

"Aw, come off! Somebody must uh slipped yuh a two-gallon jug uh something. I've rode the range about as long as you've cooked on it, and I never knowed a man to go without his supper yet, just because he come in late. I betche yuh dassent stand and say that before Chip, yuh blamed old Dutch—" Just there, Happy Jack dodged and escaped getting more than a third of the basin of water which came splashing out of the tent.

The group under the willows could no longer lie at ease while they listened; they jumped up and moved closer, just as a crowd always does surge nearer and nearer to an exciting centre. They did not, however, interfere by word or deed.

"If yuh wasn't just about ready t' die of old age and general cussedness," stormed Happy Jack, "I'd just about kill yuh for that." This, however, is a revised version and not intended to be exact. "I want my supper, and I want it blame quick, too, or there'll be a dead Dutchman in camp. No, yuh don't! You git out uh that tent and lemme git in, or—" Happy Jack had the axe in his hand by then, and he swung it fearsomely and permitted the gesture to round out his sentence.

Perhaps there would have been something more than words between them, for even a Happy Jack may be goaded too far when he is hungry; but Chip, who had been washing out some handkerchiefs down by the creek, heard the row and came up, squeezing a ball of wet muslin on the way. He did not say much when he arrived, and he did not do anything more threatening than hang the handkerchiefs over the guy-ropes to dry, tying the corners to keep the wind from whipping them away up the coulee, but the result was satisfying—to Happy Jack, at least. He ate and was filled, and Patsy retired from the fray, sullenly owning defeat for that time at least. He went up the creek out of sight from camp, and he stayed there until the dusk was so thick that his big, white-aproned form was barely distinguishable in the gloom when he returned.

At daylight he was his old self, except that he was perhaps a trifle gruff when he spoke and a good deal inclined to silence, and harmony came and abode for a season with the Flying U.

Patsy had for years cooked for Jim Whitmore and his "outfit"; so many years it was that memory of the number was never exact, and even the Old Man would have been compelled to preface the number with a few minutes of meditation and a "Lemme see, now; Patsy's been cooking for me—eighty-six was that hard winter, and he come the spring—no, the fall before that. I know because he like to froze before we got the mess-house chinked up good—I'll be doggoned if Patsy ain't gitting *old!*" That was it, perhaps: Patsy was getting old. And old age does not often sweeten one's temper, if you notice. Those angelic old men and old ladies have nearly all been immortalized in stories and songs, and the unsung remainder have nerves and notions and rheumatism and tongues sharpened by all the disappointments and sorrows of their long lives.

Patsy never had been angelic; he had always been the victim of more or less ill-timed humor on the part of the Happy Family, and the victim of hunger-sharpened tempers as well. He had always grumbled and rumbled Dutch profanity when they goaded him too hard, and his amiability had ever expressed itself in juicy pies and puddings rather than in words. On this roundup, however, he was not often amiable and he was nearly always rumbling to himself. More than that, he was becoming resentful of extra work and bother and he sometimes permitted his resentment to carry him farther than was wise.

To quarrel with Patsy was rapidly becoming the fashion, and to gossip about him and his faults was already a habit; a habit indulged in too freely, perhaps, for the good of the camp. Isolation from the world brings small things into greater prominence than is normally their due, and large troubles are born of very small irritations.

For two days there was peace of a sort, and then Big Medicine, having eaten no dinner because of a headache, rode into camp about three o'clock and headed straight for the mess-wagon, quite as if he had a right that must not be questioned. Custom did indeed warrant him in lunching without the ceremony of asking leave of the cook, for Patsy even in his most unpleasant moods had never until lately tried to stop anyone from eating when he was hungry.

On this day, however, Big Medicine unthinkingly cut into a fresh-baked pie set out to cool. There were other pies, and in cutting one Big Medicine was supported by precedent; but Patsy chose to consider it an affront and snatched the pie from under Big Medicine's very nose.

"You fellers vot iss always gobbling yet, you iss quit it alreatty!" rumbled Patsy, bearing the pie into the tent with Big Medicine's knife still lying buried in the lately released juice. "I vork und vork mine head off keeping you fellers filled oop tree times a day alreatty; I not vork und vork to feed you effery hour, py cosh. You go mitout till supper iss reaty for you yet."

Big Medicine, his frog-like eyes standing out from his sun-reddened face, stared agape. "Well, by cripes!" He hesitated, looking about him; but whether his search was for more pie or for moral support he did not say. Truth to tell, there was plenty of both. He reached for another pie and another knife, and he grinned his wide grin at Irish, who had just come up. "Dutchy's trying to run a whizzer," he remarked, cutting a defiant gash clean across the second pie. "What do yuh know about that?"

"He's often took that way," said Irish soothingly. "You don't want all that pie—give me about half of it."

Big Medicine, his mouth too full for coherent utterance, waved his hand and his knife toward the shelf at the back of the mess-wagon where three more pies sat steaming in the shade. "Help yourself," he invited juicily when he could speak.

Those familiar with camp life in the summer have perhaps observed the miraculous manner in which a million or so "yellow-jackets" will come swarming around when one opens a can of fruit or uncovers the sugar jar. It was like that. Irish helped himself without any hesitation whatever, and he had not taken a mouthful before Happy Jack, Weary and Pink were buzzing around for all the world like the "yellow-jackets" mentioned before. Patsy buzzed also, but no one paid the slightest attention until the last mouthful of the last pie was placed in retirement where it would be most appreciated. Then Weary became aware of Patsy and his wrath, and turned to him pacifically.

"Oh, yuh don't want to worry none about the pie," he smiled winningly at him. "Mamma! How do you expect to keep pies around this camp when yuh go right on making such good ones? Yuh hadn't ought to be such a crackajack of a cook, Patsy, if you don't want folks to eat themselves sick."

If any man among them could have soothed Patsy, Weary would certainly have been the man; for next to Chip he was Patsy's favorite. To say that he failed is only one way of making plain how great was Patsy's indignation.

"Aw, yuh made 'em to be eat, didn't yuh?" argued Happy Jack. "What difference does it make whether we eat 'em now or two hours from now?"

Patsy tried to tell them the difference. He called his hands and his head to help his rage-tangled tongue and he managed to make himself very well understood. They did not argue the fine point of gastronomic ethics which he raised, though they felt that his position was not unassailable and his ultimate victory not assured.

Instead, they peered into boxes and cans which were covered, gleaned a whole box of seeded raisins and some shredded cocoanut just to tease him and retired to wrangle ostentatiously over their treasure trove in the shade of the bed-tent, leaving Patsy to his anger and his empty tins.

Other men straggled in, drifted with the tide of their appetites to the cook-tent, hovered there briefly and retired vanquished and still hungry. They invariably came over to the little group which was munching raisins and cocoanut and asked accusing questions. What was the matter with Patsy? Who had put him on the fight like that? and other inquiries upon the same subject.

Just because they were all lying around camp with nothing to do but eat, Patsy was late with his supper that night. It would seem that he dallied purposely and revengefully, and though the Happy Family flung at him taunts and hurry-up orders, it is significant that they shouted from a distance and avoided coming to close quarters.

Just how and when they began their foolish little game of imitation broncho-fighting does not matter. When work did not press and red blood bubbled they frequently indulged in "rough-riding" one another to the tune of much taunting and many a "Bet yuh can't pitch *me* off!" Before supper was called they were hard at it and they quite forgot Patsy.

"I'll give any man a dollar that can ride me straight up, by cripes!" bellowed Big Medicine, going down upon all fours by way of invitation.

"Easy money, and mine from the start!" retorted Irish and immediately straddled Big Medicine's back. Horses and riders pantingly gave over their own exertions and got out of the way, for Big Medicine played bronk as he did everything else: with all his heart and soul and muscles, and since he was strong as a bull, riding him promised much in the way of excitement.

"Yuh can hold on by my collar, but if yuh choke me down I'll murder yuh in cold blood," he warned Irish before he started. "And don't yuh dig your heels in my ribs neither, or I'm liable to bust every bone yuh got to your name. I'm ticklish, by cripes!"

"I'll ride yuh with my arms folded if yuh say so," Irish offered generously. "Move, you snail!" He struck Big Medicine spectacularly with his hat, yelled at the top of his voice and the riding began immediately and tumultuously.

It is very difficult to describe accurately and effectively the evolutions of a horse when he "pitches" his worst and hardest. It is still more difficult to set down in words the gyrations of a man when he is playing that he is a broncho and is trying to dislodge the fellow upon his back. Big Medicine reared and kicked and bellowed and snorted. He came down upon a small "pin-cushion" cactus and was obliged to call a recess while he extracted three cactus spines from his knee with his smallest knife-blade and some profanity.

He rolled down his trousers' leg, closed his knife and tossed it to Pink for fear he might lose it, examined critically a patch of grass to make sure there were no more cacti hidden there and bawled: "Come on, now, I'll sure give yuh a run for your money *this* time, by cripes!" and began all over again.

How human muscles can bear the strain he put upon his own must be always something of a mystery. He described curves in the air which would sound incredible; he "swapped ends" with all the ease of a real fighting broncho and came near sending Irish off more than once. Insensibly he neared the cook-tent, where Patsy so far forgot himself as to stand just without the lifted flap and watch the fun with sour interest.

"Ah-h *want* yuh!" yelled Big Medicine, quite purple but far from surrender, and gave a leap.

"Go *get* me!" shouted Irish, whipping down the sides of his mount with his hat.

Big Medicine answered the taunt by a queer, twisted plunge which he had saved for the last. It brought Irish spread-eagling over his head, and it landed him fairly in the middle of Patsy's great pan of soft bread "sponge"—and landed him upon his head into the bargain. Irish wriggled there a moment and came up absolutely unrecognizable and a good deal dazed. Big Medicine rolled helplessly in the grass, laughing his big, bellowing laugh.

It was straight into that laugh and the great mouth from where it issued, that Patsy, beside himself with rage at the accident, deposited all the soft dough which was not clinging to the head and face of Irish. He was not content with that. While the Happy Family roared appreciation of the spectacle, Patsy returned with a kettle of meat and tried to land that neatly upon the dough.

"Py cosh, if dat iss der vay you wants your grub, py cosh, dat iss der vay you gets it alreatty!" he brought the coffee-boiler and threw that also at the two, and followed it with a big basin of stewed corn.

Irish, all dough as he was, went for him blindly and grappled with him, and it was upon this turbulent scene which Chip looked first when he rode up. The Happy Family crowded around him gasping and tried to explain.

"They were doing some rough-riding—"

"By golly, Patsy no business to set his bread dough on the ground!"

"He's throwed away all the supper there is, and I betche—"

"Mamma! Yuh sure missed it, Chip. You ought—"

"By cripes, if that Dutch—"

"Break away there, Irish!" shouted Chip, dismounting hurriedly. "Has it got so you must fight an old man like that?"

"Py cosh, I'll fight mit him alreatty! I'll fight mit any mans vat shpoils mine bread. Maybe I'm old yet but I ain't dead yet und I could fight—" The words came disjointedly, mere punctuation points to his wild sparring.

It was plain that Irish, furious though he was, was trying not to hurt Patsy very much; but it took four men to separate them for all that. When they had dragged Irish perforce down to the creek by which they had camped, and had yelled to Big Medicine to come on and feed the fish, quiet should have been restored—but it was not.

Patsy was, in American parlance, running amuck. He was jumbling three languages together into an indistinguishable tumult of sound and he was emptying the cook-tent of everything which his stout, German muscles could fling from it. Not a thing did he leave that was eatable and the dishes within his reach he scattered recklessly to all the winds of heaven. When one venturesome soul after another approached to calm him, he found it expedient to duck and run to cover. Patsy's aim was terribly exact.

The Happy Family, under cover or at a safe distance from the hurtling pans, cans and stove wood, caressed sundry bumps and waited meekly. Irish and Big Medicine, once more disclosing the features God had given them, returned by a circuitous route and joined their fellows.

"Look at 'em over there—he's emptying every grain uh rolled oats on the ground!" Happy Jack was a "mush-fiend." "Somebody better go over and stop 'im—"

"You ain't tied down," suggested Cal Emmett rather pointedly, and Happy Jack said no more.

Chip, usually so incisively clear as to his intentions and his duties, waited irresolutely and dodged missiles along with the rest of them. When Patsy subsided for the very good reason that there was nothing else which he could throw out, Chip took the matter up with him and told him quite plainly some of the duties of a cook, a few of his privileges and all of his limitations. The result, however, was not quite what he expected. Patsy would not even listen.

"Py cosh, I not stand for dose poys no more," he declared, wagging his head with its shiny crown and the fringe of grizzled hair around the back. "I not cook grub for dat Irish und dat Big Medicine und Happy Jack und all dose vat cooms und eats mine pies und shpoils mine pread und makes deirselves fools all der time. If dose fellers shtay on dis camp I quits him alreatty." To make the bluff convincing he untied his apron, threw it spitefully upon the ground and stamped upon it clumsily, like a maddened elephant.

"Well, quit then!" Chip was fast losing his own temper, what with the heat and his hunger and a general distaste for camp troubles. "This jangling has got to stop right here. We've had about enough of it in the last month. If you can't cook for the outfit peaceably—" He did not finish the sentence, or if he did the distance muffled the words, for he was leading his horse back to the vicinity of the rope corral that he might unsaddle and turn him loose.

He heard several voices muttering angrily, but his wrath was ever of the stiff-necked variety so that he would not look around to see what was the matter. The tumult grew, however, until when he did turn he saw Patsy stalking off across the prairie with his hat on and his coat folded neatly over his arm, and Irish and Big Medicine fighting wickedly in the open space between the two tents. He finished unsaddling and then went stalking over to quell this latest development.

"They're trying to find out who was to blame," Weary informed him when he was quite close. "Bud hasn't got much tact: he called Irish a dough-head. Irish didn't think it was true humor, and he hit Bud on the nose. He claims that Bud pitched him into that dishpan uh dough with malice aforethought. Better let 'em argue the point to a finish, now they're started. It's black eyes for the peacemaker—you believe *me*."

While the dusk folded them close and the nighthawks swooped from afar, the Happy Family gathered round and watched them fight. Chip and Weary thoughtfully went into the bed-tent and got the guns which were stowed away in the beds of the combatants, so that when their anger reached the killing point they must let it bubble harmlessly until the fires which fed it went cold. Which was exceeding wise of the two, for Big Medicine and Irish did get to that very point and raged all over the camp because they could not shoot each other.

The hottest battle must perforce end sometime, and so the camp of the Flying U did at last settle into some semblance of calm. Irish rolled his bed, saddled a horse and rode off toward town, quite as if he were going for good and all. Big Medicine went down to the creek for the second time that evening to wash away the marks of strife, and when he returned he went straight to bed without a word to anyone. Patsy was gone, no man knew whither, and the cook-tent was as nearly wrecked as might be.

"Makes me think uh that time we had the ringtailed tiger in camp," sighed Andy Green, shaking sand out of the teakettle so that it could be refilled.

"By golly, I'd ruther have a whole band uh tagers than this fighting bunch," Slim affirmed earnestly. Slim was laboring sootily with the stove-pipe which Patsy had struck askew with a stick of wood.

Outside, Happy Jack was protesting in what he believed to be an undertone against being installed in Patsy's place. "Aw, that's always the way! Anything comes up, it's 'Happy, you git in and rustle some chuck.' *I* ain't no cook—or if I be they might pay me cook's wages. I betche there ain't another man in camp would stand for it. Somebody's got to take that bacon down to the creek and wash it off, if yuh want any meat for supper. There ain't no time to boil beef. If I'd a been boss uh this outfit, I betche no blame cook on earth would uh made rough-house like Patsy done." But no one paid the slightest attention to Happy Jack, having plenty to think of and to do before they slept.

Not even the sun, when it shone again, could warm their hearts to a joy in living. Happy Jack cooked the breakfast, but his coffee was weak and his biscuits "soggy," and Patsy had managed to make the butter absolutely uneatable with sand; also they were late and Chip was surly over the double loss of cook and cow-boy. Happy Jack packed food and dishes in much the same spirit which Patsy had shown the night before, climbed sullenly to the high seat, gathered up the reins of the four restive horses, released the brake and let out a yell surcharged with all the bitterness bottled within his soul. *He* had not done anything to precipitate the trouble. Beyond eating half a pie he had been an innocent spectator, not even taking part in the rough-riding. Yet here he was, condemned to the mess-wagon quite as if he were to blame for Patsy's leaving. The eyes of Happy Jack gazed gloomily upon the world, and his driving seemed a reckless invitation to disaster. "I betche I'll make 'em good and sick uh *my* cooking!" he plotted while he went rattling and bumping over the untrailed prairie.

He succeeded so well that two days later Chip gave a curt order or two and headed his wagons, horses and his lean-stomached bunch of riders for Dry Lake, passing by even the Flying U coulee in his haste. Just outside the town, upon the creek which saves the inhabitants from dying of thirst or *delirium tremens,* he left the wagons with Happy Jack, Slim and one alien to set up camp and rode dust-dogged to the little, red depot.

The telegram which went speeding to Great Falls and to a friend there was brief, but it was eloquent and not quite flattering to Happy Jack. It read like this:

"JOHN G. SCOTT,

"The Palace, Great Falls.

"For God's sake send me a cook by return train; must deliver goods or die hard.

"BENNETT, Flying U."

Whether the cook must die hard, or whether he meant the friend, Chip did not trouble to make plain. Telegrams are bound by such rigid limitations, and he had gone over the ten-word rate as it was. But he told Weary to receive the cook, be he white or black, have him restock the mess-wagon to his liking and then bring the outfit to the ranch, when Chip would again take it in hand. He said that he was going home to get a square meal, and he mentioned Happy Jack along with several profane words. "Johnny Scott will send a cook, and a good one,"; he added hopefully. "Johnny never threw down a friend in his life and he never will. And say, Weary, if he wires, you collect the message and act accordingly. I'm going to have a decent supper, to-night!" He was riding a good horse and there was no reason why he should be late in arriving, especially if he kept the gait at which he left town.

In two hours Weary, Pink and Andy Green were touching hat-brims over a telegram from Johnny Scott—a telegram which was brief as Chip's, and more illuminating:

"CHIP BENNETT,

"Dry Lake.

"Kidnaped Park hotel chef best cook in town will be on next train.

J.G. SCOTT."

"Sounds good," mused Andy, reading it for the fourth time. "But there's thirteen words in that telegram, if yuh notice."

"I wish yuh wouldn't try to butt in on Happy Jack's specialty," Weary remonstrated, folding the message and slipping it inside the yellow envelope. "If this is the same jasper that cooked there a month ago, we're going to eat ourselves plumb to death; a better meal I never laid away inside me than the one I got at the Park Hotel when I was up there last time. Come on over to the hotel and eat; their chuck isn't the best in the world, but it could be a lot worse and still beat Happy Jack to a jelly."

PART TWO

The whole Happy Family—barring Happy Jack, who was sulking in camp because of certain things which had been said of his cooking and which he had overheard—clanked spurs impatiently upon the platform and waited for the arrival of the train from the West. When at last it snorted into town and nosed its way up to the platform they bunched instinctively and gazed eagerly at the steps which led down from the smoker.

A slim little man in blue serge, a man with the complexion of a strip of rawhide and the mustache of a third-rate orchestra leader, felt his way gingerly down by the light of the brakeman's lantern, hesitated and then came questioningly toward them, carrying with some difficulty a bulky suitcase.

"It's him, all right," muttered Pink while they waited.

The little man stopped apologetically before the group, indistinct in the faint light from the office window. Already the train was sliding away into the dark. "Pardon," he apologized. "I am looking for the U fich flies."

"This is it," Weary assured him gravely. "We'll take yuh right on out to camp. Pretty dark, isn't it? Let me take your grip—I know the way better than you do." Weary was not in the habit of making himself a porter for any man's accommodation, but the way back to where they had left the horses was dark, and the new cook was very small and slight. They filed silently back to Rusty Brown's place, invited the cook in for a drink and were refused with soft-voiced regret and the gracious assurance that he would wait outside for them.

Weary it was, and Pink to bear him company, who piloted the stranger out to camp and showed him where he might sleep in Patsy's bed. Patsy had left town, the Happy Family had been informed, with the declaration often repeated that he was "neffer cooming back alreatty." He had even left behind him his bed and his clothes rather than meet again any member of the Flying U outfit.

"We'd like breakfast somewhere near sunrise," Weary told the cook at parting. "Soon as the store opens in the morning, we'll drive in and you can stock up the wagon; we're pretty near down to

cases, judging from the meals we have been getting lately. Hope yuh make out all right."

"I will do very nicely, I thank you," smiled the new cook in the light of the lantern which stood upon the fireless cook-stove. "I wish you good-night, gentlemen, and sweet dreams of loved ones."

"Say, he's a polite son-of-a-gun," Pink commented when they were riding back to town. "'The U fich flies'—that's a good one! What is he, do you thing? French?"

"He's liable to be most anything, and I'll gamble he can build a good dinner for a hungry man. That's the main point," said Weary.

At daybreak Weary woke and heard him humming a little tune while he moved softly about the cook-tent and the mess-wagon, evidently searching mostly for the things which were not there, to judge from stray remarks which interrupted the love song. "Rolled oat—I do not find him," he heard once. And again: "Where the clean towels they are, that I do not discover." Weary smiled sleepily and took another nap.

The cook's manner of announcing breakfast was such that it awoke even Jack Bates, notoriously a sleepy-head, and Cal Emmett who was almost as bad. Instead of pounding upon a pan and lustily roaring *Grub-pi-i-ile!* in the time-honored manner of roundup cooks, he came softly up to the bed-tent, lifted a flap deprecatingly and announced in a velvet voice:

"Breakfast is served, gentlemen."

Andy Green, whose experiences had been varied, sat up and blinked at the gently swaying flap where the cook had been standing. "Say, what we got in camp?" he asked curiously. "A butler?"

"By golly, that's the way a cook *oughta* be!" vowed Slim, and reached for his hat.

They dressed hastily and trooped down to the creek for their morning ablutions, and hurried back to the breakfast which waited. The new cook was smiling and apologetic and anxious to please. The Happy Family felt almost as if there were a woman in camp and became very polite without in the least realizing that they were not behaving in the usual manner, or dreaming that they were unconsciously trying to live up to their chef.

"The breakfast, it is of a lacking in many things fich I shall endeavor to remedy," he assured them, pouring coffee as if he were serving royalty. He was dressed immaculately in white cap and apron, and his mustache was waxed to a degree which made it resemble a cat's whiskers. The Happy Family tasted the coffee and glanced eloquently at one another. It was better than Patsy's coffee, even; and as for Happy Jack—

There were biscuits, the like of which they never had tasted before. The bacon was crisp and delicately brown and delicious, the potatoes cooked in a new and enticing way. The Happy Family showed its appreciation as seemed to them most convincing: They left not a scrap of anything and they drank two cups of coffee apiece when that was not their habit.

Later, they hitched the four horses to the mess-wagon, learned that the new cook, though he deeply regretted his inefficiency, did not drive anything. "The small burro," he explained, "I ride him, yes, and also the automobile drive I when the way is smooth. But the horses I make not acquainted with him. I could ride upon the elevated seat, yes, but to drive the quartet I would not presume."

"Happy, you'll have to drive," said Weary, his tone a command.

"Aw, gwan!" Happy Jack objected, "He rode out here all right last night—unless somebody took him up in front on the saddle, which I hain't heard about nobody doing. A cook's supposed to do his own driving. I betche—"

Weary went close and pointed a finger impressively. "Happy, you *drive*," he said, and Happy Jack turned without a word and climbed glumly up to the seat of the mess-wagon.

"Well, are yuh coming or ain't yuh?" he inquired of the cook in a tone surcharged with disgust.

"If you will so kindly permit, it give me great pleasure to ride with you and to make better friendship. It now occurs to me that I have not yet introduce. Gentlemen, Jacques I have the honor to be name. I am delighted to meet you and I hope for pleasant association." The bow he gave the group was of the old school.

Big Medicine grinned suddenly and came forward. "Honest to grandma, I'm happy to know yuh!" he bellowed, and caught the cook's hand in a grip that sent him squirming upon his toes. "These here are my friends: Happy Jack up there on the wagon, and Slim and Weary and Pink and Cal and Jack Bates and Andy Green—and there's more scattered around here, that don't reely count except when it comes to eating. We like you, by cripes, and we like your cookin' fine! Now, you amble along to town and load up with the best there is—huh?" It occurred to him that his final remarks might be construed as giving orders, and he glanced at Weary and winked to show that he meant nothing serious. "So long, Jakie," he added over his shoulder and went to where his horse waited.

Jacques—ever afterward he was known as "Jakie" to the Flying U—clambered up the front wheel and perched ingratiatingly beside Happy Jack, and they started off behind the riders for the short mile to Dry Lake. Immediately he proceeded to win Happy from his glum aloofness.

"I would say, Mr. Happy, that I should like exceeding well to be friends together," he began purringly. "So superior a gentleman must win the admiration of the onlooker and so I could presume to question for advisement. I am experience much dexterity for cooking, yes, but I am yet so ignorant concerning the duties pertaining to camp. If the driving of these several horses transpire to pertain, I will so gladly receive the necessary instruction and endeavor to fulfil the accomplishment. Yes?"

Happy Jack, more in stupefaction at the cook's vocabulary than anything else, turned his head and took a good look at him. And the trustful smile of Jakie went straight to the big, soft heart of him and won him completely. "Aw, gwan," he adjured gruffly to hide his surrender. "I don't mind driving for yuh. It ain't that I was kicking about."

"I thank you for the so gracious assurement. If I transgress not too greatly, I should like for inquire what is the chuck for which I am told to fill the wagon. I do not," he added humbly, "understand yet all the language of your so glorious country, for fich I have so diligently study the books. Words I have not yet assimilated completely, and the word chuck have yet escape my knowledge."

"Chuck," grinned Happy Jack, "is grub."

"Chuck, it is grub," repeated Jakie thoughtfully. "And grub, that is—Yes?"

Happy Jack struggled mentally with the problem. "Well, grub is grub; all the stuff yuh eat is grub. Meat and flour and coffee and—"

"Ah, the light it dawns!" exclaimed Jakie joyously. "Grub it is the supply of provision fich I must obtain for camping, yes? I thank you so graciously for the information; because," he added a bit wistfully, "that little word chuck she annoy me exceeding and make me for not sleep that I must grasp the meaning fich elude. I am now happy that I do not make the extensive blunder for one small word fich I apprehend must be a food fich I must buy and perhaps not to understand the preparation of it. Yes? It is the excellent jest at the expense of me."

"There ain't much chuck in camp," Happy observed helpfully, "so yuh might as well start in and get anything yuh want to cook. The outfit is good about one thing They don't never kick on the stuff yuh eat. The cook always loads up to suit himself, and nobody don't ask questions or make a holler—so long as there's plenty and it's good."

Jakie listened attentively, twisting his mustache ends absently. "It is simply that I purchase the supplies fich I shall choose for my judgment," he observed, to make quite sure that he understood. "I am to have *carte blanche*, yes?"

"Sure, if yuh want it," said Happy Jack. "Only they might not keep it here. Yuh can't get *everything* in a little place like this." It is only fair to Happy Jack to state that he would have understood the term if he had seen it in print. It was the pronunciation which made the words strange to him.

Jakie looked puzzled, but being the soul of politeness he made no comment— perhaps because Happy Jack was at that moment bringing his four horses to a reluctant stand at the wide side-door of the store.

"The horses, they are of the vivacious temperament, yes?" Jakie had scrambled from the seat to within the door and was standing there smiling appreciatively at the team.

"Aw, they're all right. You go on in—I guess Weary's there. If he ain't, you go ahead and get what yuh want. I'll be back after awhile." Thirst was calling Happy Jack; he heeded the summons and disappeared, leaving the new cook to his own devices.

So, it would seem, did every other member of the Flying U. Weary had been told that Miss Satterly was in town, and he forgot all about Jakie in his haste to find her. No one else seemed to feel any responsibility in the matter, and the store clerks did not care what the Flying U outfit had to eat. For that reason the chuck-wagon contained in an hour many articles which were strange to it, and lacked a few things which might justly be called necessities.

"Say, you fellows are sure going to live swell," one of the clerks remarked, when Happy Jack finally returned. "Where did yuh pick his nibs? Ain't he a little bit new and shiny?"

"Aw, he's all right," Happy Jack defended jealously. "He's a real *chaff*, and he can build the swellest meals yuh ever eat. Patsy can't cook within a mile uh him. And *clean*—I betche *he* don't keep his bread-dough setting around on the ground for folks to tromp on." Which proves how completely Jakie had subjugated Happy Jack.

That night—nobody but the horse-wrangler and Happy Jack had shown up at dinner-time—the boys of the Flying U dined luxuriously at their new-made camp upon the creek-bank at the home ranch, and ate things which they could not name but which pleased wonderfully their palates. There was a salad to tempt an epicure, and there was a pudding the like of which they had never tasted. It had a French name which left them no wiser than before asking for it, and it looked, as Pink remarked, like a snowbank with the sun shining on it, and it tasted like going to heaven.

"It makes me plumb sore when I think of all the years I've stood for Patsy's slops," sighed Cal Emmett, rolling over upon his back because he was too full for any other position—putting it plainly.

"By golly, I never knowed there was such cookin' in the world," echoed Slim. "Why, even Mis' Bixby can't cook that good."

"The Countess had ought to come down and take a few lessons," declared Jack Bates emphatically. "I'm going to take up some uh that pudding and ask her what she thinks of it."

"Yuh can't," mourned Happy Jack. "There ain't any left—and I never got more'n a taste. Next time, I'm going to tell Jakie to make it in a wash tub, and make it full; with some uh you gobblers in camp—"

He looked up and discovered the Little Doctor approaching with Chip. She was smiling a friendly welcome, and she was curious about the new cook. By the time she had greeted them all and had asked all the questions she could think of and had gone over to meet Jakie and to taste, at the urgent behest of the Happy Family, a tiny morsel of salad which had been overlooked, it would seem that the triumph of the new cook was complete and that no one could possibly give a thought to old Patsy.

The Little Doctor, however, seemed to regret his loss—and that in the face of the delectable salad and the smile of Jakie. "I do think it's a shame that Patsy left the way he did," she remarked to the Happy Family in general, being especially careful not to look toward Big Medicine. "The poor old fellow *walked* every step of the way to the ranch, and Claude"—that was Chip's real name—"says it was twenty-five or six miles. He was so lame and he looked so old and so—well, friendless, that I could have *cried* when he came limping up to the house! He had walked all night, and he got here just at breakfast time and was too tired to eat.

"I dosed him and doctored his poor feet and made him go to bed, and he slept all that day. He wanted to start that night for Dry Lake, but of course we wouldn't let him do that. He was wild to leave, however, so J.G. had to drive him in the next day. He went off without a word to any of us, and he looked so utterly dejected and so—so *old*. Claude says he acted perfectly awful in camp, but I'm sure he was sorry for it afterwards. J.G. hasn't got over it yet; I believe he has taken it to heart as much as Patsy seemed to do. He's had Patsy with him for so long, you see—he was like one of the family." She stopped and regarded the Happy Family a bit anxiously. "This new cook is a very nice little man," she added after a minute, "but after all, he isn't Patsy."

The Happy Family did not answer, and they refrained from looking at one another or at the Little Doctor.

At last Big Medicine brought his big voice into the awkward silence. "Honest to grandma, Mrs. Chip," he said earnestly, "I'd give a lot right now to have old Patsy back—er—just to have *around*, if it made him feel bad to leave. I reckon maybe that was my fault: I hadn't oughta pitched quite so hard, and I had oughta looked where I was throwin' m' rider. I reelize that no cook likes to have a fellow standin' on his head in a big pan uh bread-sponge, on general principles if not on account uh the bread. Uh course, we've all knowed old Patsy to take just about as great liberties himself with his sponge—but we've got to recollect that it was *his* dough, by cripes, and that pipe ashes ain't the same as a fellow takin' a shampoo in the pan. No, I reelize that I done wrong, and I'm willin' to apologize for it right here and now. At the same time," he ended dryly, "I will own that I'm dead stuck on little Jakie, and I'd ruther ride for the Flying U and eat Jakie's grub than any other fate I can think of right now. Whilst I'm sorry for what I done, yuh couldn't pry me loose from Jakie with a stick uh dynamite—and that's a fact, Mrs. Chip."

The Little Doctor laughed, pushed back her hair in the way she had, glanced again at the unresponsive faces of the original members of the Happy Family and gave up as gracefully as possible.

"Oh, of course Patsy's an old crank, and Jakie's a waxed angel," she surrendered with a little grimace. "You think so now, but that's because you are being led astray by your appetites, like all men. You just wait: You'll be *homesick* for a sight of that fat, bald-headed, cranky old Patsy bouncing along on the mess-wagon and swearing in Dutch at his horses, before you're through. If you're not so completely gone over to Jakie that you will eat nothing but what he has cooked, come on up to the house. The Countess is making a twogallon freezer of ice-cream for you, and she has a big pan of angel cake to go with it! You don't deserve it—but come along anyway." Which was another endearing way of the Little Doctor's—the way of sweetening all her lectures with something very nice at the end.

The Happy Family felt very much ashamed and very sorry that they could not feel kindly toward Patsy, even to please the Little Doctor. They sincerely wanted to please her and to have her unqualified approval; but wanting Patsy back, or feeling even the slightest regret that he was gone, seemed to them a great deal too much to ask of them. Since this is a story of cooks and of eating, one may with propriety add, however, that the invitation to ice cream and angel cake, coming though it did immediately after that wonderful supper of Jakie's, was accepted with alacrity and their usual thoroughness of accomplishment; not for the world would they have offended the Little Doctor by declining so gracious an invitation—the graciousness being manifested in her smile and her voice rather than in the words she spoke—leaving out the enchantment which hovers over the very name of angel cake and ice cream. The Happy Family went to bed that night as complacently uncomfortable as children after a Christmas dinner.

Not often does it fall to the lot of a cowboy to have served to him stuffed olives and lobster salad with mayonnaise dressing, French fried potatoes and cream puffs from the mess-tent of a roundup outfit. During the next week it fell to the lot of the Happy Family, however. When the salads and the cream puffs disappeared suddenly and the smile of Jakie became pensive and contrite, the Happy Family, acting individually but unanimously, made inquiries.

"It is that I no more possess the fresh vegetables, nor the eggs, gentlemen," purred Jakie. "Many things of a deliciousness must I now abstain because of the absence of two, three small eggs! But see, one brief arrival in the small town would quickly remedy, yes? It is that we return with haste that I may buy more of the several articles for fich I require?" He spread his small hands appealingly.

"By golly, *Patsy* never had no eggs—" began Slim traitorously.

"Aw, gwan! Patsy never fed yuh like Jakie does, neither!" Happy Jack was heart and soul the slave of the chef. "If Chip don't care, I'll ride over to Nelson's and git some eggs. Jakie said he'd make some more uh that pudding if he had some. It ain't but six or seven miles."

"Should you but obtain the juvenile hen, yes, I should be delighted to serve the chicken salad for luncheon. It is the great misfortune that the fresh vegetable are not obtain, but I will do the best and substitute with a cleverness fich will conceal the defect—yes?" Jakie's caps and aprons had lost their first immaculate freshness, but his manner was as royally perfect as ever and his smile as wistfully friendly.

"Well, I'll ask Chip about it," Happy Jack yielded.

Eggs and young chickens were of a truth strange to a roundup in full blast, but so was a chef like Jakie, and so were the salads, stuffed olives and cream puffs; and the white caps and the waxed mustache and the beautiful flow of words and the smile. The Happy Family was in no condition, mentally or digestively, to judge impartially. A month ago they would have whooped derision at the suggestion of riding anywhere after fresh eggs and "juvenile hens," but now it seemed to them very natural and very necessary. So much for the demoralization of expert cookery and white caps and a smile.

Chip also seemed to have fallen under the spell. It may have been that the heavenly peace which wrapped the Flying U was, in his mind, too precious to be lightly disturbed. At any rate he told Happy Jack briefly to "Go ahead, if you want to," and so left unobstructed the path to the chicken salad and cream puffs. Happy Jack wiped his hands upon an empty flour sack, rolled down his shirtsleeves and hurried off to saddle a horse.

Happy Jack did not realize that he was doing two thirds of the work about the cook-tent, but that was a fact. Because Jakie could not drive the mess-wagon team, Happy Jack had been appointed his assistant. As assistant he drove the wagon from one camping place to another, "rustled" the wood, peeled the potatoes, tended fires and washed dishes, and did the thousand things which do not require expert hands, and which, in time of stress, usually falls to the horse-wrangler. Jakie was ever smiling and always promising, in his purring voice, to cook something new and delicious, and left with the leisure which Happy's industry gave him, he usually kept his promise.

"Now, Mr. Happy," he would smile, "I am agreeable to place the confidence in your so gracious person that you prepare the potatoes, yes? And that you attend to the boiling of meat and the unpacking and arrangement of those necessary furnishings for fich you possess the great understanding. And I shall prepare the so delicious dessert of the floating island, what you call in America. Yes? Our friends will have the so delightful astonishment when they arrive. They shall exclaim and partake joyously, is it not? And for your reward, Mr. Happy, I shall be so pleased to set aside a very extensive portion of the delicious floating island, so that you can eat no more except you endanger your handsome person from the bursting. Yes?" And oh, the smile of him!

A man of sterner stuff than Happy Jack would have fallen before such guile and would have labored willingly—nay, gladly in the service of so delightful a diplomat as Jakie. Except for that willing service, Jakie would have been quite overwhelmed by the many and peculiar duties of a roundup cook. He would have been perfectly helpess before the morning and noon packing of dishes and food, and the skilful haste necessary to unpack and prepare a meal for fifteen ravenous appetites within the time limit would have been utterly impossible. Jakie was a chef, trained to his profession in well-appointed kitchens and with assistance always at hand; which is a trade apart from cooking for a roundup crew.

Happy Jack, in the fulness of time, returned with the eggs. That is, he returned with six eggs and a quart or two of a yellowish mixture thickly powdered with shell. He took the pail to Jakie and he saw the seraphic smile fade from his face and an unpleasant glitter creep into his eyes.

"It is the omelet fich you furnish, yes? The six eggs, they will not make the pudding. The omelet—I do not perceive yet the desirableness of the omelet. And the juvenile hen—yes?"

"Aw, they wouldn't sell no chickens." Happy Jack's face had gone long and scarlet before the patent displeasure of the other. "And my horse was scared uh the bucket and pitched with me."

Jackie looked again into the pail, felt gingerly the yellow mess and discovered one more egg which retained some semblance of its original form. "The misfortune distresses me," he murmured. "It is that you return hastily, Mr. Happy, and procure other eggs fich you will place unbroken in my waiting hands, yes?"

Happy Jack mopped his forehead and glanced at the sun, burning hotly down upon the prairie. They had made a short move that day and it was still early. But the way to Nelson's and back had been hot and tumultuous and he was tired. For the first time since his abject surrender to the waxed smile, Happy Jack chafed a bit under the yoke of voluntary servitude. "Aw, can't yuh cook something that don't take so many eggs?" he asked in something like his old, argumentative tone.

The unpleasant glitter in the eyes of Jakie grew more pronounced; grew even snaky, in the opinion of Happy Jack. "It is that I am no more permitted the privilege of preparing the food for fich I have the judgment, yes?" His voice purred too much to be convincing. "It is that I am no more the chef to be obeyed by my servant?"

"Aw, gwan! I ain't anybody's servant that I ever heard of!" Happy Jack felt himself bewilderedly slipping from his loyalty. What had come over Jakie, to act like this? He walked away to where there was some shade and sat down sullenly. Jakie's servant, was he? Well! "The darned little greasy-faced runt," he mumbled rebelliously, and immediately felt the better for it.

Two cigarettes brought coolness and calm. Happy Jack wanted very much to lie there and take a nap, but his conscience stirred uneasily. The boys were making a long circle that day and would come in with the appetites—and the tempers—of wolves. It occurred to Happy Jack that their appetites were much keener than they had ever been before, and he sat there a little longer while he thought about it; for Happy Jack's mind was slow and tenacious, and he hated to leave a new idea until he had squeezed it dry of all mystery. He watched Jakie moving in desultory fashion about the tent—but most of the time Jakie stayed inside.

"I betche the boys ain't gitting enough old stand-by-yuh chuck," he decided at length. "Floatin' island and stuffed olives—for them that likes stuffed olives— and salad and all that junk *tastes* good—but I betche the boys need a good feed uh beans!" Which certainly was brilliant of Happy Jack, even if it did take him a full hour to arrive at that conclusion. He got up immediately and started for the cook-tent.

"Say, Jakie," he began before he was inside, "ain't there time enough to boil a pot uh beans if I make yuh a good fire? I betche the boys would like a good feed—"

"A-a-hh!" Happy Jack insisted afterward that it sounded like the snarling of a wolf over a bone. "Is it that you come here to give the orders? Is it that you *insult*?" Followed a torrent of molten French, as it were. Followed also Jakie, with the eyes of a snake and the toothy grin of a wild animal and with a knife which Happy Jack had never seen before; a knife which caught the sunlight and glittered horridly.

Happy Jack backed out as if he had inadvertently stirred a nest of hornets. Jakie almost caught him before he took to his heels. Happy never waited to discover what the new cook was saying, or whether he was following or remaining at the tent. He headed straight for the protection of the horse-wrangler, who watched his cavvy not far away, and his face was the color of stale putty.

The horse-wrangler saw him coming and came loping up to meet him. "What's eating yuh, Happy?" he inquired inelegantly.

"Jakie—he's gone nutty! He come at me with a knife, and he'd uh killed me if I'd stayed!" Happy Jack pantingly recovered himself. "I didn't have no time ta git my gun," he added in a more natural tone, "or I'd uh settled him pretty blame quick. So I come out to borrow yourn. I betche *I'll* have the next move."

The horse-wrangler grinned heartlessly. "I reckon he's about half shot," he said, sliding over in the saddle and getting out the inevitable tobacco sack and papers. "Old Pete Williams rode past while you were gone, loaded to the guards and with a bottle uh whisky in each saddle-pocket and two in his coat. He gave me a drink, and then he went on and stopped at camp. He was hung up there for quite a spell, I noticed. I didn't *see* him pass any uh the vile liquor to little Jakie, but—" he twirled a blackened match stub in his fingers and then tossed it from him.

"Aw, gwan! Jakie wouldn't touch nothing when he was in town," Happy Jack objected. "I betche he's gone crazy, or else—"

"Well," interrupted the horse-wrangler, "I've told yuh what I know and all I know. Take it or leave it." He rode back to turn the lead-horse from climbing a ridge where he did not want the herd to follow. He did not lend Happy Jack his gun, and for that reason—perhaps—Jakie remained alive and unpunctured until the first of the riders came loping in to camp.

The first riders happened to be Pink and Big Medicine. They were met by a tearful, contrite Jakie—a Jakie who seemed much inclined to weeping upon their shirt-fronts and to confessing all his sins, particularly the sin of trying to carve Happy Jack. That perturbed gentleman made his irate appearance as soon as he found that reinforcements had arrived.

Big Medicine disengaged himself from the clinging arms of the chef, sniffed suspiciously and wiped away the tears from his vest. "Well, say," he bellowed in his usual manner of trying to make all Chouteau County hear what he had to say, "I ain't t' blame if he got away on yuh. Yuh hadn't ought to uh done it—or else yuh oughta made a clean job of it sos't we could hang yuh proper. Supper ready?"

"It is that the supply of eggs is inadequate," wept Jakie, steadying himself against the tent-pole while he wiped his eyes upon his apron. "Because of it I could not prepare the floating island—and without the dessert I have not the heart to prepare the dinner, yes? It is that I am breaking of the heart that I assail the good friend of me. Oh, Mr. Happy, it is that I crave pardon!"

Happy Jack came near taking to his heels again when he saw Jakie start for him; he did back up hastily, and his evident reluctance to embrace and forgive started afresh the tears of remorse. Jakie wailed volubly and, catching Pink unaware, he wept upon his bosom.

Others came riding in, saw the huddle before the mess-tent and came up to investigate. With every fresh arrival Jakie began anew his confession that he had attempted to murder his good friend, Mr. Happy, and with every confession he wept more copiously than before.

The Happy Family tacitly owned itself helpless. A warlike cook they could deal with. A lazy cook they could kick into industry. A weeping, wailing, conscience-stricken cook, a cook who steadfastly refused to be comforted, was an absolutely new experience. They told him to buck up, found that he only broke out anew, threatened, cajoled and argued. Jakie clung to whoever happened to be within reach and mixed the English language unmercifully.

"Happy, you'll have to forgive him," said Weary at last. "Go tell him yuh don't feel hard towards him. We want some supper."

"Aw, gwan. I *ain't* forgive him, and I never will. I—"

Big Medicine stepped into the breach. With his face contorted into a grin to crimple one's spine, with a voice to make one's knees buckle, he went up to Happy Jack and thrust that horrible grin into Happy's very face. "By cripes, you forgive Jakie, and you do it quick!" he thundered. "Think you're going to ball up the eating uh the whole outfit whilst you stand around acting haughty? Why, by cripes, I've killed men in the Coconino County for *half* what you're doing! You'll wish, by cripes, that Jakie *had* slit your hide; you'll consider that woulda been an easy way out, before I git half through with yuh. You walk right up and shake hands with him, and you tell him that yuh love him to death and are his best friend and always will be! Yuh *hear* me?"

Happy Jack heard. The Happy Family considerately moved aside and left him a clear path, and they looked on without a word while he took Jakie's limp hand, muttered tremulously, "Aw, fergit it, Jakie. I know yuh didn't mean nothing by it, and I forgive yuh," and backed away again.

Jakie wept, this time with gratitude. They got him inside a tent, unrolled his bed and persuaded him to lie down upon it. They searched the mess-box, found all that was left of a quart bottle of whisky, took it outside and divided it gravely and appreciatively among themselves. There was not much to divide.

Happy Jack took charge of the pots and pans, with the whole Happy Family to help him hurry supper, while Jakie forgot his woes in sleep and the sun set upon a quiet camp.

Next morning, Jakie was up and cooking breakfast at the appointed time, and the camp felt that the incident of the evening before might well be forgotten. The coffee was unusually good that morning, even for Jakie. He was subdued, was Jakie, and his soft, brown eyes were humble whenever they met the eyes of Happy Jack. His smile was infrequent and fleeting, and his voice more deprecating than ever. Aside from these minor changes everything seemed the same as before the sheepmen had stopped at camp.

That afternoon, however, came an aftermath in the shape of Happy Jack galloping wildly out to where the others were holding a herd and "cutting out." He was due to come and help, so nobody paid any attention to his haste, though it was his habit to take his time. He shot recklessly by the outer fringes of the "cut" and yelled in a way to stampede the whole bunch. "Jakie's *dying*," he shouted, wild-eyed. "He's drunk up all the lemon extract and most uh the v'nilla before I could stop him!"

Chip and Weary, riding in hot haste to the camp, found that it was true as far as the drinking was concerned. Jakie was stretched upon his back breathing unpleasantly, and beside him were two flat bottles of half-pint size, one empty and the other very nearly so; the tent and Jakie's breath reeked of lemon and vanilla. Chip sent back for help.

For the second time the Flying U roundup was brought to an involuntary pause because of its cook. There was but one thing to do, and Chip did it. He broke camp, loaded Jakie into the bed-wagon, and headed at a gallop for Dry Lake in an effort to catch the next train for Great Falls. Whether he sent Jakie to the hospital or to the undertaker was a question he did not attempt to answer; one thing was certain, however, that he must send him to one of those places as soon as might be.

That night, just before the train arrived, he sent another telegram to Johnny Scott at rush rates. He said simply:

> "Send another cook immediately this one all in am returning him in baggage coach this train.
>
> > "C. BENNETT."

Just after midnight he went to the station and received an answer, which is worth repeating:

> "C. BENNETT, Dry Lake: Supply cooks running low am sending only available don't kill this one or may have to go without season on cooks closed fine attached to killing, running with dogs or keeping in captivity this one drunk look for him in Pullman have bribed porter.
>
> > J.G. SCOTT."

It was sent collect, which accounts perhaps for the facetious remarks which it contained.

It was morning when that train arrived, because it was behind time for some reason, but Chip, Weary, Pink and Big Medicine were at the depot to meet it. The new cook having been reported drunk, they wanted to make sure of getting him off the train in case he proved unruly. They were wise in the ways of intoxicated cooks. They ran to the steps of the only Pullman on the train and were met by the grinning porter.

"Yas sah, he's in dah—but Ah cyan't git 'im off, sah, to save mah soul," he explained toothily. "Ah put 'im next de front end, sah, but he's went to sleep and Ah cyan't wake 'em up, an' Ah cyan't tote 'em out nohow. Seems lak he weighs a ton!"

"By cripes, *we'll* tote him out," declared Big Medicine, pushing ahead of Chip in his enthusiasm. "You hold the train, and we'll git 'im. Show us the bunk."

The porter pointed out the number and retreated to the steps that he might signal the conductor. The four pushed up through the vestibule and laid hold upon the berth curtains.

"Mamma!" ejaculated Weary in a stunned tone. "Look what's in here, boys!"

They thrust forward their heads and peered in at the recumbent form.

"Honest to grandma—it's old Patsy!" The voice of Big Medicine brought heads out all along down the car.

"Come out uh that!" Four voices made up the chorus, and Patsy opened his eyes reluctantly.

"Py cosh, I not cook chuck for you fellers ven I'm sick," he mumbled dazedly.

"Come out uh that, you damned Dutch belly-robber!" bawled Big Medicine joyously, and somewhere behind a curtain a feminine shriek was heard at the shocking sentence.

Four pairs of welcoming hands laid hold upon Patsy; four pairs of strong arms dragged him out of the berth and through the narrow aisle to the platform. The conductor, the head brakeman and the porter were chafing there, and they pulled while the others pushed. So Patsy was deposited upon the platform, grumbling and only half sober.

"Anyway, we've got him back," Weary remarked with much satisfaction the next day when they were once more started toward the range land. "When Irish blows in again, we'll be all right."

"By cripes, yuh just give me a sight uh that Irish once, and he'll *come*, if I have to rope and drag 'im!" Big Medicine took his own way of intimating that he held no grudge. "Did yuh hear what Patsy said, by cripes, when he was loading up the chuck-wagon at the store? He turned in all that oil and them olives and *anchovies*, yuh know, and he told Tom t' throw in about six cases uh blueberries. I was standin' right handy by, and he turns around and scowls at me and says: 'Py cosh, der vay dese fellers eats pie mit derselves, I have to fill oop der wagon mit pie fruit alreatty!' And then the old devil turns around with his back to me, but yuh can skin me for a coyote if I didn't ketch a grin on 'is face!"

They turned and looked back to where Patsy, seated high upon the mess-wagon, was cracking his long whip like pistol shots and swearing in Dutch at his four horses as he came bouncing along behind them.

"Well, there's worse fellers than old Patsy," Slim admitted ponderously. "I don't want no more Jakie in mine, by golly."

"I betche Jakie cashes in, with all that lemon in him," prophesied Happy Jack with relish. "Dirty little Dago—it'd serve him right. Patsy wouldn't uh acted like that in a thousand years."

They glanced once more behind them, as if they would make sure that the presence of Patsy was a reality. Then, with content in their hearts, they galloped blithely out of the lane and into the grassy hills.

THE END.

Lector House believes that a society develops through a two-fold approach of continuous learning and adaptation, which is derived from the study of classic literary works spread across the historic timeline of literature records. Therefore, we aim at reviving, repairing and redeveloping all those inaccessible or damaged but historically as well as culturally important literature across subjects so that the future generations may have an opportunity to study and learn from past works to embark upon a journey of creating a better future.

This book is a result of an effort made by Lector House towards making a contribution to the preservation and repair of original ancient works which might hold historical significance to the approach of continuous learning across subjects.

HAPPY READING & LEARNING!

LECTOR HOUSE LLP
E-MAIL: lectorpublishing@gmail.com

9 789353 442323

Printed in July 2019
by Rotomail Italia S.p.A., Vignate (MI) - Italy

IT € 10,60

THE HAPPY FAMILY

LECTOR HOUSE LLP
E-MAIL: lectorpublishing@gmail.com

LECTOR HOUSE

ISBN 9789353442323

9 789353 442323